MORRIS
INTERNATIONAL
AIRPORT

Travels with a pop star and his people

DICKIE FELTON

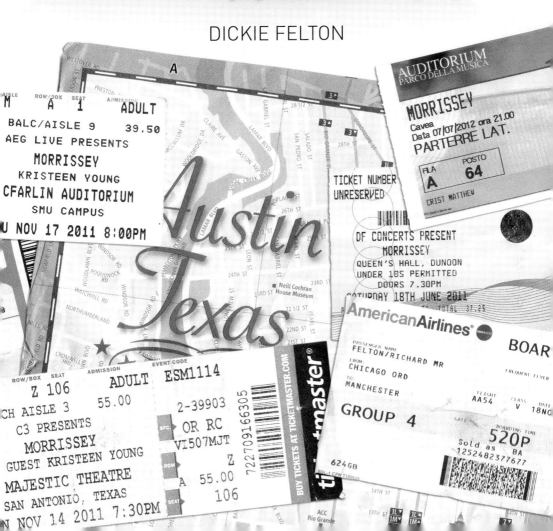

AUDITORIUM
PARCO DELLA MUSICA

MORRISSEY
Cavea
Data 07/07/2012 ora 21.00
PARTERRE LAT.

FILA	POSTO
A	64

CRIST MATTHEW

M A 1 ADULT
AISLE ROW/BOX SEAT ADMISSION
BALC/AISLE 9 39.50
AEG LIVE PRESENTS
MORRISSEY
KRISTEEN YOUNG
CFARLIN AUDITORIUM
SMU CAMPUS
U NOV 17 2011 8:00PM

TICKET NUMBER
UNRESERVED

DF CONCERTS PRESENT
MORRISSEY
QUEEN'S HALL, DUNOON
UNDER 18S PERMITTED
DOORS 7.30PM
SATURDAY 18TH JUNE 2011

American Airlines

PASSENGER NAME
FELTON/RICHARD MR
FROM
CHICAGO ORD
TO
MANCHESTER

FLIGHT CLASS DATE
AA54 V 18NO

GROUP 4

BOAR

GATE BOARDING TIME
520P
Sold as BA
1252482377677

Z 106 ADULT ESM1114
ROW/BOX SEAT ADMISSION EVENT CODE
CH AISLE 3 55.00
C3 PRESENTS
MORRISSEY
GUEST KRISTEEN YOUNG
MAJESTIC THEATRE
SAN ANTONIO, TEXAS
N NOV 14 2011 7:30PM

2-39903
OR RC
VI507MJT
Z
A 55.00
106

ticketmaster
BUY TICKETS AT TICKETMASTER.COM

Words and photographs copyright Dickie Felton, 2012,
(unless otherwise stated).

First published in Great Britain in 2012 by
Bootle Bruiser Books Limited.

Email for publisher queries: bootlebruiser@yahoo.com

1

The moral right of the author has been asserted.

ISBN: 978-0-9562157-1-0

Design and layout by Sundog Creative Limited, Formby, Merseyside.
01704 876393 shine@sundogcreative.co.uk

Photographs on introduction and author pages by Mark McNulty

www.dickiefelton.com

Vivamos

10 Morrissey concerts

10 towns

5 countries

12,000 miles

Were you there?

2011

SCOTLAND:
Friday 17 June
Inverness Ironworks
Capacity 1,000
(285 miles on three trains)

Saturday 18 June
Dunoon Queens Hall
Capacity 1,000
(173 miles on two trains and one ferry)

ENGLAND:
Saturday 25 June
York Barbican
Capacity 1,800
(102 miles train)

Monday 27 June
Bradford St George's Hall
Capacity 1,800
(140 miles round-trip car)

ISLE OF MAN:
Monday 1 August
Douglas Villa Marina
Capacity 1,614
(180 miles round-trip ferry)

AMERICA:
Monday 14 November
Majestic Theatre, San Antonio, Texas
Capacity 2,311
(4,839 miles via train, plane, assorted taxis and Greyhound bus)

Tuesday 15 November
Bass Hall, Austin, Texas
Capacity 2,800
(77 miles Greyhound bus)

Thursday 17 November
McFarlin Memorial Auditorium, Dallas, Texas
Capacity 2,386
(200 miles Amtrak)

(Journey home from Dallas to Liverpool: 4,823 miles. Two planes, two trains, one 53a bus)

2012

ITALY:
Saturday 7 July
Cavea Auditorium, Rome
Capacity 3,000
(2,100 mile round-trip plane)

ENGLAND:
Saturday 28 July
Manchester Arena
Capacity 20,000
(70 mile round-trip train)

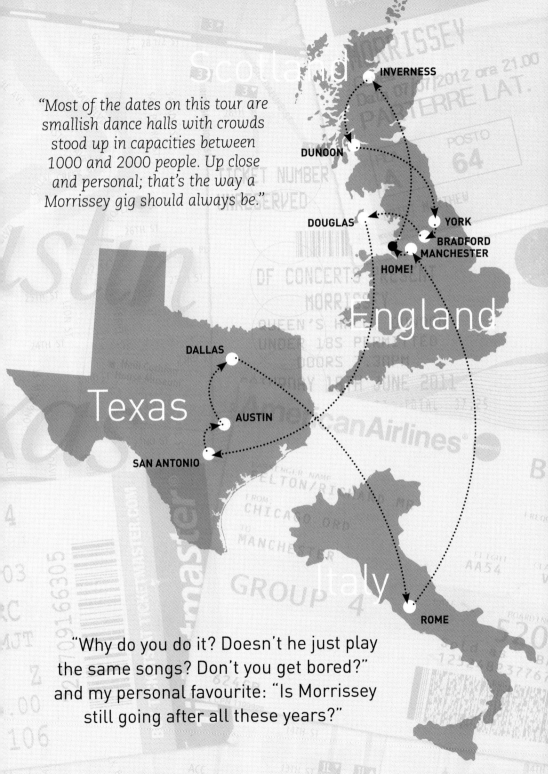

"Most of the dates on this tour are smallish dance halls with crowds stood up in capacities between 1000 and 2000 people. Up close and personal; that's the way a Morrissey gig should always be."

Scotland

INVERNESS

DUNOON

DOUGLAS

YORK

BRADFORD

MANCHESTER

HOME!

England

Texas

DALLAS

AUSTIN

SAN ANTONIO

Italy

ROME

"Why do you do it? Doesn't he just play the same songs? Don't you get bored?" and my personal favourite: "Is Morrissey still going after all these years?"

Introduction

I've trekked to so many Morrissey concerts over the last 20 years, I've lost count of the actual number. Blackburn, Bradford, Belfast, Blackpool. I think the total might be more than 70. Hartlepool, Halifax, Llandudno, London, Madrid, Manchester. Oh I dunno, maybe it's nearer 80.

When I first saw Morrissey at Aberdeen Capitol Theatre in 1991 I was transfixed. His amazing voice, his passionate lyrics, his quiff, his Doc Martins. This was the man for me. After that very first night I just wanted to get to as many of his concerts as possible. But as the years and tours went by I became as interested in Morrissey's hardcore fan base as I did in the music legend himself. And it became apparent that despite my impressive attendance record at Morrissey gigs it paled into insignificance compared to other fans.

I've always been taken by Morrissey's fans' style; their look, their tattoos, their tales of devotion. The huge journeys routinely travelled to his gigs by fans are unique in music. His fans seem more akin to a partizan football crowd than typical concert-goers. Then there's this league of nations at Morrissey concerts; you hear American, Australian, Italian and French accents at his gigs.

But who are these people? In the summer of 2011, when Morrissey embarked on a tour of far off places, I decided to follow. My aim was not just to experience the greatest living singer in action but to get under the skin of his most passionate fans too. I planned to attend ten Morrissey concerts in ten very different places, to chronicle and capture this most dedicated band of followers. To try and understand this movement, this Moz Army. Why are they all on this journey?

Liverpool

Saturday 7 November 2009, Echo Arena, Liverpool, England

Saturday 7 November 2009, Echo Arena, Liverpool, England

Fans from America, fans from Ainsdale. Faces I haven't seen for years. Beers, banter, the atmosphere oozes anticipation. We bounce into the Baltic Fleet pub close to Liverpool's Echo Arena. Tonight is the night. Morrissey in my city.

Once inside the venue 9,000 of us prepare for our idol's biggest UK date of the year. The standing section is rammed. Great craic and Morrissey due on the attack. What could possibly go wrong? Darkness descends, he marches on stage and shouts into the microphone: "It's Saturday, it's raining, it's Liverpool and it's perfect." First song *This Charming Man*, greeted by a mass Merseyside roar. "This is amazing," I shout. Second song, *Black Cloud*, marked by a missile, a bottle? A glass? I was too busy dancing to really notice, but it strikes quiff and suit. And then he's off. Goodnight, Liverpool.

It had been the shortest Morrissey gig I'd ever been to; kept to a tragically trim six minutes. There's nothing like a quick set to keep the masses wanting more (or less). A chorus of boos reverberates around the venue as it's announced Morrissey is not coming back. The hordes traipse back into town, one cursing "that miserable Manc".

Monday 9 November 2009

BBC Radio Merseyside's Breakfast Show presenter, Tony Snell, quizzes me, (local lad and Morrissey devotee), on the debacle. "Tony, it's fair to say that Morrissey's Liverpool Echo Arena concert was not a tremendous success. But I don't blame him for abandoning the concert. How would anyone like a pint thrown at them? It would've been great if he had dusted himself down and come back on stage. But it just didn't happen."

The overriding feeling is one of shame. Shame that it was in my city that Morrissey was assaulted on what should have been an amazing end to the tour. The venue pledges that investigations will be launched and attempts made to catch the missile thrower.

Thursday 12 November 2009

I pick up the Mirror newspaper. Writer Brian Reade gives a frank appraisal of Saturday's non-concert in his column. Under an image of the moment pint pot connects with quiff is the headline: "*Time to call it a day Morrissey: You old wet*".

Reade: "I donned my best student gear...ready for an hour and a half bopping" until "some over-excited tool threw a half-full plastic glass at the stage which bounced off Morrissey's head. I just thought back to my days of regular gigging when singers expected their head to take bucketfuls of spit and many more objects besides. Then realised those singers were in their 20s and so was I. Morrissey's now in his 50s and so am I. Probably best if we both call this rock 'n' roll lark a day, eh Mozza?"

Shoving down the tabloid, I reflect on the crap end to my 2009 Morrissey odyssey. I'd watched him play everywhere from a tiny sports hall in Omagh (with no bar and no thrown glasses) to Great Yarmouth where he played at the end of an ageing pier that was more accustomed to Chuckle Brothers and Chubby Brown than *This Charming Man*. In the last few months I'd seen Morrissey play Belfast, Glasgow, Manchester, Liverpool Empire and London's Alexandra Palace.

And now Liverpool Echo Arena with fans picking up the pieces of two songs instead of 22. I was gutted the *Swords* tour had been slain, and I couldn't end my 2009 tour adventure in such dismal circumstances. I'd been to nine Morrissey shows during the tour and each had been a revelation. I read Reade again, then put the paper down. I pick up the phone and book a ticket to see Morrissey a week on Monday in Dublin's National Stadium.

Monday 23 November 2009
Dublin National Stadium, Ireland

For me, the best way of experiencing the whole phenomena that is a Morrissey gig is to travel. There's no thrill in seeing him sing at the bottom of the garden. You need to grab your bag, some fine wine, and hit the road.

The most straightforward way to reach Dublin from Liverpool is to fly but I'm more interested in quality and experience of journey than speed. Budget plane travel is banned: the check-in, the cramped legroom, the security, the scratchcard up-selling...it ain't for me. To see Morrissey play Dublin's National Stadium I was going to rail-sail. This meant an early start, three trains from Merseyside over to North Wales and then a fast ferry to the Emerald Isle.

Jimmy, the ticket guy at Blundellsands and Crosby train station, looked lost. He stared at his tiny computer screen, unconvinced I would make it: "Er, it should be do-able mate, but the ferry you want to catch is not showing up on my screen. You could take a chance and get yourself over to Holyhead and see if there are any sailings..." I needed to get to Dublin for 7pm to see Morrissey again and banish Liverpool's bottle-gate.

Mark Smith - the modern day patron saint of rail travel - eulogises about turning our backs on road and air in favour of rail and sea. His excellent book *The Man in Seat 61* shows how easy it is to get pretty much anywhere by letting the train take the strain. And Ireland is a perfect destination for green travel from England. Smith writes: "Fed up with flying? More volcanic ash on its way? It's time to swap stressful flights or cramped coaches on eyesore motorways for a relaxed train ride through the English countryside and along the beautiful Welsh coast, then by luxurious superferry across the Irish Sea. £38 (€45), any day, any date, buys you a 'SailRail' train and ferry ticket from London or any rail station in Britain to Dublin. It's the traditional way to reach Ireland, an environmentally-friendly alternative to a flight. Bring a bottle of your favourite wine along (try doing that on Ryanair), sit back with a good book and enjoy the ride..."

And so I was taking Smith's good advice. I was trekking to see my hero and saving the planet at the same time. But as I sat on three hours' worth of trains, the weather turned for the worse. I got to Holyhead to find my planned lunchtime ferry cancelled. I looked out from the quayside to the Irish Sea - it was wet, windy and rough - and this was why sailings were disrupted.

This meant another eternity killing time in this North Wales town until late afternoon. I was going to be cutting this Morrissey show fine. I walked around Holyhead town centre, stopping for a veggie fry-up and to log on at an internet cafe. I avoided pubs on the premise that a nice pint (or three) awaited on the Jonathan Swift fast ferry.

Soon I was aboard, travelling 39 knots and enjoying a choppy two hour crossing. I decided to pay an extra £15 to upgrade to a spacious lounge. It was the best £15 I'd ever spent. I reclined in my spacious blue leather armchair which overlooked the bow and felt like Skipper Felton. I'd sail this ship alone.

Sixty four miles (and a few complementary red wines) later I was on the blustery deck as we sailed into Dublin. It was now early teatime, dark and absolutely freezing. Cranes, container ships and Dublin docks reminded me of U2 videos and weekends of my past in this tremendous city. I dumped my gear in Barnacles hostel which is the cheapest place to stay in one of the most expensive streets in Europe. Then that sensation that money can't buy: "I'm actually here, in Temple Bar, in Dublin, to see Morrissey, tonight."

I meet two Morrissey fans who I know, Kev and Mark. We jump a cab up towards the National Stadium. In the pub opposite the venue, Kev introduces me to Martin - the singer out of fantastic Irish band Sack.

Once inside the venue I'm shocked at its size, or lack of it. Don't be misled by the words 'National Stadium', this is basically a small boxing venue more accustomed to bouts not bands and it's packed.

Morrissey enters the fray shortly after 9pm. What follows is one hour 20 minutes of perfection. A wonderful gig. *Why Don't You Find Out For Yourself* and *The Loop* highlights. The noise, the camaraderie, the singer in splendid form. No pints thrown and Morrissey feeling all at home: "*All my family are from this city.*"

Afterwards I sell 12 copies of my first book - *The Day I Met Morrissey*. I enter a nearby pub full of Morrissey fans ecstatic at the gig. I've now lost Kev and Mark. Until a text: "I'm in Bruxelles Bar with Boz - join us for a drink." I hail a cab - my head and heart still ringing from the concert. Down some stairs to a darkened bar and a wall of loud, booming music. I'm feeling tired. After all, this day started in Liverpool and now it's midnight in Dublin. This had had been my tenth and last Morrissey gig of the year. Now a dimly lit and very rowdy Bruxelles bar, tucked off Grafton Street, provides the scene for the post show nightcap.

There, leaning against the wall is Kev and none other than Boz Boorer - Morrissey's guitarist. A man responsible for writing the music to some of Morrissey's most attractive hits. I join them for a few ales. It's great, though we can barely hear a word each other are saying. I congratulate Boz on a fantastic gig. "We won't talk about the Liverpool show" I say.

Boz tells us how he will travel to the next date on the tour - Seattle - early. Moz and the rest of the band would follow him a day later. Boz, the model professional, wants to get to Seattle asap: "To get over the jet lag". Boz is one of the most affable guys you can meet. A true gent, tremendous company and one of the greatest guitarists in music.

It's now pushing 1am. Struggling to sup an ounce more Guinness, it's time to call it a night. Kevin and Boz, in great spirits, also succumb to tiredness. The last European date of Morrissey's 2009 Swords tour ends for me on Grafton Street and the freezing air of the Emerald Isle.

Interlude 1

"I have been a Smiths/Morrissey fan for at least 20 years. But for different reasons, I've never had the chance to see him sing live. Several years ago I decided to make a life list (I'm a big fan of lists) and one of the items on it is to see Morrissey live. I promised myself that the next time he toured I would see him, no matter how far I had to travel to do so.

"I nearly hyperventilated when I saw he'd announced British dates. I literally squealed in excitement. I should probably note that I work for the Canadian federal government in a building populated with stuffy public servants and I was sitting in my office at the time. I didn't care. I also didn't waste a moment. I bought tickets to the Hop Farm festival and told myself I would worry about the details later.

"Several months later, I'm only two weeks away from crossing it off my list and I'm so excited I can hardly stand it. This is a monumental and defining moment in my life. I raised my daughter listening to The Smiths and Morrissey, as I will with any future children I have. His music is a part of my life and always will be."

Carrie, Canada

Inverness

Friday 17 June 2011,
Ironworks, Inverness, Scotland

Friday 18 March 2011

Credit cards lined up, mobile phone glued to ear, landline on redial, computer screen freezing. Panic stricken and in a hot sweat, I shout in desperation and disbelief: "How can York Barbican be sold out already?" Like dominos falling, the series of Morrissey dates just announced for Scotland and England are selling out one after the other. Morrissey tickets always go on sale on a Friday, usually when I should be somewhere else.

What is it that makes getting concert tickets so bloody difficult? Inverness, sold out; Bradford, sold out; York, sold out. Sod it, I'll try Dunoon - I've never even heard of it. Where is it exactly? 'Click, click, click' on my computer mouse. What's my credit card security code? What, only seats left? Perth? Some left for Perth? What date is that? What's my name? Help, this is driving me mad. And then a frenzied glance at my watch. I need to be at an important work meeting and I'm ten minutes late.

Friday 20 May 2011

I email guesthouses in Dunoon, Scotland: "Hello. Do you have any rooms for Saturday June 18th? I'm coming to Dunoon for the Morrissey concert. I'm after a single room. Thanks, Dickie Felton." 8.38pm: "Hi, sorry, we don't. Thank you for your enquiry. Regards James. Dhaillinglodge, Dunoon." 8.39pm: "Sorry Dickie we are fully booked for 18 June. Alec Jones, Rosscairn Hotel, Dunoon."

Saturday 21 May 2011

So I got on the phone instead: "Hello. Have you any rooms for Saturday 18th June?" The Cedars Guesthouse: "Aye, Morrissey? You know I could have filled this guesthouse three or four times over. It seems the whole world is heading for Dunoon for this concert. So, sorry no, I don't have any rooms. If you didn't find anywhere to stay you could always get the last ferry back to Gourock but I think it leaves at ten to nine. Why don't you try the Scottish Tourist Board for vacancies? Anyway, good luck."

This was not going well. So I turn to Google Maps to scour the streets of Dunoon virtually. Street after street I roam looking for "x" to mark the spot. And then between something called 'Artisan Cake Toppers' and a loch was the Ardtully Hotel.

The Ardtully has no website. Get this, in 2011 a hotel on mainland Britain without a website. You cannot be serious? Surely the first rule of the hotel trade is to let people know that you actually exist? For the first time since 1982 I actually have to ring directory enquiries to trace a phone number.

After three rings, The Ardtully's Angela answered and was set to save my life: "You want a room for June 18th? That will be for the Morrissey concert. Let me see. Ah yes, we have one left. We've have had lots of people enquire about this. I can tell you that our little town is thrilled to have Morrissey visit, even though none of us have ever really heard of him."

Me: "Well, Morrissey is a music legend. He used to be in a group called The Smiths. He tends to play venues a little bit off the beaten track and that's why he's coming to Dunoon. You have a room? Thank God for that."

Angela: "What style is Morrissey's music?" Me: "I guess it's indie, or pop, or rock. Er, I'm not really sure. He's a bit like Elvis Presley or one of the crooners from the 1960s. He has this perception of being a bit miserable but a lot of his songs are really funny and uplifting. People are travelling from around the world for this concert. People just love him. So, anyway, shall I email my bank card details?"

Laughter from Angela: "A cheque sent in the post will be fine," more giggles: "No. We don't use email here." I think I'm going to like Dunoon and The Ardtully.

Thursday 16 June 2011

It's like a scene from an episode of *Whatever Happened to The Likely Lads?* where the two characters try to avoid learning the result of an important England football match. Morrissey is on stage in Perth, Scotland for the opening date of his 2011 UK tour and I'm not there. Instead I'm sat at home in Liverpool avoiding the internet, Twitter and email.

Tomorrow I travel to Inverness for the second date of the tour and want the setlist to be a surprise. So, as I resist the temptation to look at Facebook for the millionth time and I wonder what's happening in Perth, a text comes through from friend Dan Gallagher: "OMG Morrissey is on stage playing *The Boy Racer! Ouija Board!* and *I Know It's Over!*"

Thanks, Dan.

Friday 17 June 2011
Ironworks, Inverness, Scotland

As the wheels on the luggage go round and round I'm conscious of waking the world. Time 5.49am and I'm dragging my case and me from pillow to platform. All trains this June head to Inverness and Dunoon.

The thrill of an early morning escape and a mouthful of cake. This is no ordinary holiday. This is a Morrissey tour. It's great to travel, to know that hours from now I'll be a world away from work. Have you ever escaped to a shipwrecked Fife? For the next few weeks I'm a rebel with a cause - get to as many Morrissey concerts as possible and squeeze in a family holiday to Paris in between.

My trip north enables me to combine two passions - travel and Morrissey. And there's no bland Wembley Arena or Manchester Evening News Arena to get to. Only the most obscure dance halls in out-of-the-way towns will do. Most of the dates on this tour are smallish dance halls with crowds stood up in capacities between 1,000 and 2,000 people. Up close and personal; that's the way a Morrissey gig should always be.

Today I'm leaving Liverpool to trek 293 miles which will take just over eight hours. A series of complex train connections await for my date with Moz at Inverness Ironworks. I need to catch the Preston train, then an Edinburgh train, before onward to Inverness. The following day I'll travel back down through Scotland via two trains and a ferry to the quiet holiday town of Dunoon to catch my second Morrissey gig in as many nights.

Of course, the downside of small venues is the manic scramble for tickets. When they went on sale three months ago I had a nightmare. I tried, I failed. After being stuck in a meeting, I surfaced to find all the tickets gone.

It's nothing new for me to miss out on Morrissey tickets. Such is demand. In 2009, for Morrissey's 50th birthday show at Manchester Apollo, I failed miserably through official ticket channels but turned up at the venue on the night anyway. Ticket touts stalked the street dressed in tracksuit bottoms and leather. In thick Manchest-urgh drawl they scowled: "Any Morrissey tickets? Buy or sell". These touts wanted £200 a ticket. A mark-up of £165.

So much for the government or anyone getting tough on ticket touting. It's a joke, it's rife and as always it's the loyal fans in desperation who pay over the odds to ensure these touts wave their hefty wads at the world. What do they buy with their spoils? Probably guns, drugs and bulldogs. Nice crowd, not. And then, out of the mist that night outside the Apollo came American Morrissey fan, Cathy McCartan with a spare ticket. Since that moment two years ago I've taken a much more radical view on getting into gigs. More often than not, someone's got a spare ticket and is not always after a king's ransom for it.

For this tour, after my complete failure going through the official ticket channels, I'd sent out a plea to key followers of our hero. Long time Morrissey fan Chris Wilde came to my rescue with a ticket for tonight's Inverness gig. He'd also put me in touch with another fan with a spare ticket for tomorrow's gig in Dunoon.

Today, when I arrive in Inverness, I need to find Chris then locate an American who I've never met who goes by the Twitter name of *Catenin* or *DailyAlice*. She apparently has my Dunoon ticket. I think her real name is Margaret. Should I have worn a pink carnation? Anyway I've got eight hours of glorious British train travel first before landing. For those without a degree in geography, Inverness is the northernmost city in the United Kingdom and lies within the Great Glen where the River Ness enters the Moray Firth. The city is home to a fantastic sounding football team: Inverness Caledonian Thistle. Regarded as the capital of the Highlands, Inverness was the scene of the 18th-century Battle of Culloden. Tonight, 265 years on, there will be a gathering of a different clan.

As I slip into my seat on the 06:57 for the first leg of my journey I wonder how many other people will be doing exactly the same as me. In the internet chat rooms there was talk of fans flying in from Europe, America and even Chile to catch this tour.

I've no problem travelling alone to Morrissey gigs. You tend to meet people. There is a unique bond between his fans. People have followed this singer through thick and thin. It is very much a gang mentality. You, me, Morrissey. We're in this together. Detractors ask "Why do you do it? Doesn't he play the same songs? Don't you get bored?" and my personal favourite: "Is Morrissey still going after all these years?" I can't understand the criticism. Following Morrissey around the UK and farther afield is exactly the same as a football supporter following AC Milan or Marine AFC.

A football fan travels great distances to watch his or her team. They journey somewhere new, they find a great pub for ales and banter, they go to the game and sing for their heroes in red or blue. That tribal feeling of travelling, experiencing something new but seeing familiar faces in unfamiliar places. The buzz of travelling away to Leeds or Levski to see your team remains despite the years. It's in your blood. And that passion, that belonging, that being part of something bigger is exactly what it means being a Morrissey fan.

Wigan, Preston, Cumbria. I stare from the train window with the vital tool of travel at my side: my iPod and Bose headphones. In keeping with my giddy mood I shuffle through tunes as my train shuffles up to Scotland. My ears enjoy Cornershop *Sleep On The Leftside*, James Horner *Back To Titanic*, Ryan Adams *Chelsea Hotel*, REM *Beat A Drum*.

"Tickets, please!" Here you go, sir. I hand over my little orange piece of card with a sense of pride and achievement. My ticket to ride is met by complete disbelief from the conductor, "You paid just £23.50 to get to Inverness?" I did. And yes, what a total bargain. What should in reality have cost £109 has cost me a fifth of that price. The key to such wonderfully cheap rail travel? Buying exceedingly early.

I feel wonderment at being on a train headed somewhere miles away, knowing that tonight I will see Morrissey in concert. Sightings of our hero in Bonnie Scotland in the last few days have sent pulses racing. A friend caught a glimpse and an autograph in Dundee. The excitement has been mounting for weeks. And then three new tracks played live on Janice Long's radio show. One song in particular, *Action Is My Middle Name*, is bursting with fantastic lyrics about us all having a date with the undertaker. It's a song about living for the moment.

The journey goes quickly. Before I know it I'm in Scotland. All change at Edinburgh for the last three hour leg. But as the train departs the rain moves in. Suddenly the northernness becomes as bleak as the banter. In the seats behind me holidaymakers from either side of the Atlantic are cementing the "special relationship" between Britain and America. The recent royal wedding has been the major talking point for the last hour.

Holidaymakers from Seattle: "Prince William looked so great. He looked a million bucks. We got up at 2am especially to watch it. We especially loved the trees in the cathedral. It was so cool. These days every American woman has the trench coat just like the one Kate Middleton wears. She's had an amazing impact on fashion. We also love Elton John."

Pass me the sick bucket. Can't someone kick them off this train on grounds of appalling taste? But my fellow Brits are beaming: "Oh we love Elton John too. He's associated with our town Watford and the football club." The discussion moves on to remedies for England's ills. "In Britain we need some national service to get some discipline back into the country." The American man: "Oh yes, I once owned a gun..." Wifey interrupts: "You were hardly a fighting machine, darling."

I feel like screaming. No, we don't need national service. No, we don't need Windsors. No we don't want Elton John. And we certainly don't want to start giving the nation firearms! Dark clouds, blackness. It's gone a bit grim. Until there's a light at the end of the tunnel in the form of six indie boys and girls who bounce aboard clutching cans of ale. Terrific - some sanity and sense at last. Disapproving looks from our Royalist Elton John fans. I suppose they'd like the six teenage passengers conscripted immediately and sent off to some far foreign land to fight in a war nobody believes in. That'll give them some discipline and sort out Britain out, won't it?

Northwards, higher up the Highlands. The scenery through the ScotRail window has a melancholic beauty. Until: "Och, the east coast of Scotland is so boring," yawns one of the indie boys. In his late teens and wearing a brown Beady Eye teeshirt, him and his pals have Liam Gallagher-style haircuts. Even the girls. I'm relieved. Their boisterous arrival means I don't have to listen to the Seattle branch of the Windsors fan club eulogising about Kate Middleton's latest look. Instead, the indie kids talk with fondness about drinking, gigging and their home city of Glasgow (or Glasgee as they call it). And after four or five hours of speaking to absolutely no-one it's time for me to open my mouth.

"So, who is the biggest band to come out of Glasgow, then?" Beady Eye fan, called Ian, responds immediately: "Dead easy: Simple Minds." Then his mate: "Hang on a minute, wa about The Proclaimers? *Sunshine on Leith*, amazing song." Ian: "The Proclaimers? Wa ya on about? They're not even from Glasgee. They come from Leith!"

I tell them how much I love Glasgow. Ian "Aye, I'm a wee bit biased. But it's the best city you will ever visit in your life." Me: "So, I guess you're off to Inverness to see Morrissey?" Ian: "Yes. We love The Smiths. Will he play many Smiths songs tonight?" I'm amazed. These cool cats probably weren't even born when The Smiths split in 1987. Their interest in Morrissey indicates how his audience isn't all late 30 somethings like me. A new, younger brigade of Moz fan is carrying the torch.

They offer me a bottle of Budweiser. That famous Scottish hospitality is not just a stereotype. It actually exists. Especially with patrons of Glasgow. I take a grateful swig then say: "I first watched Morrissey in 1991 in Aberdeen and I bet you guys weren't even born at that time?" They all burst out laughing. "You're proper old, aren't you?" says Ian, "But you're reasonably cool with it." "Cheers guys!" clinking of beer bottles all round. With such great company, the last hour or so of the journey flies by.

Welcome to Inverness. Like all great train stations, the railway station is in the centre of town. It stands in the shadow of the Royal Highland Hotel. I make my entrance and turn right along the main drag towards tonight's venue - the Ironworks. To my right a few pubs. And in a short while they'll be all mine to explore ahead of the main event.

The Ironworks is a little more than 500 yards from the train station on Academy Street. I turn a bend and the first person I see is a young man in his 20s in dark denim, turned-up jeans and a quiff. It's a sight that confirms I'm headed in the right direction. That "I'm here" back among Morrissey fans and the same familiar faces for the first time since Dublin National Stadium 19 months ago.

The clan is gathered, slumped on walls and pavement a full six hours before Morrissey is due on stage. It's all about getting your position in the queue early to ensure a front row spot for tonight's gig. This is a familiar sight at Morrissey concerts. The most ardent fans, sometimes referred to as the *Irregular Regulars*, arrive early to claim their places on the front rail. This ensures that they are as close to Morrissey as they possibly can be.

I see another fan, in lighter denim with an even bigger quiff. And then I see Chris Wilde, who like me is of a certain age and therefore has no hair at all. "Chris! Great to see you again." To me Chris Wilde is a legend in Morrissey fan circles. The softly spoken Aston Villa fan has been a regular face at gigs for decades. I'd go as far as to say he's as familiar a sight on these occasions as Morrissey himself. Chris is handing out specially homemade badges to fans to commemorate the tour. They feature Moz with a cat on his head. They look fantastic. Mine is on lapel immediately.

Chris greets me with a hug and my ticket for the gig tonight. He also points me in the direction of another fan who has a spare ticket for Morrissey's sold-out gig in Bradford, a week Monday.

Chris is extremely well connected in the Morrissey fan circle. If this was Italian football, Chris would be among the head ultras: one of the top boys and faces on *Curva Moz*. He was at Morrissey's gig last night in Perth: "It was a great gig, Dickie, but a strange gig. The setlist was…"

"Stop!" I scream. "I don't want to know what songs he plays, Chris. I'm trying to keep it a surprise." Chris: "It's a fascinating setlist. Strange even. I'll leave it at that. You'll see what I mean later. I won't spoil it for you."

Margaret Dale from Fresno, California, is standing all alone at the rear of the venue next to Morrissey's red Jumbocruiser tour bus. I owe her a big thanks. She has me a ticket for tomorrow night's gig in Dunoon. Wearing a Happy Martyr teeshirt (Boz Boorer and Alex Lusty's band), Margaret tells me how she'll be in Britain for two weeks and will attend eight Morrissey concerts. She's travelled a staggering 5,000 miles to be stood in this car park wasteland in the hope of a brush with her hero. I ask how many times she's seen Morrissey in concert: "Not enough times." I'm interested to know how Margaret finds the time to travel all this way and follow the tour for two weeks.

Margaret: "I'm a vet. I think I'm the only employed person here. I know a few fans who just ditched their jobs to be here on the tour. But I can't quit my job as I need the money. I've worked every holiday so when Moz tours I know I have the time and the money to go."

Me: "You must be looking forward to seeing some of the tourist sights while you are in Britain?"

Margaret: "Not really, no. This is my first vacation in 20 years. I have no idea what Britain looks like. All I will see for the next two weeks is the sidewalk and then the shows. I will wait for Morrissey and stand in line. That's how it has to be. If I get a handshake from him it will be worth it. People do call me obsessive and it's a label I'm proud to wear."

I leave Margaret and wander to the front of the Ironworks. I can't help noticing Inverness residents doing double takes as they pass in their cars. They see lots of quiffs, lots of denim, and must surely be asking themselves: "What on earth is going on here?"

Suddenly there's a scent of confessionals and Catholic churches as I speak to Frenchman Guillaume, 38, and his partner Ani. The aroma is Comme Des Garçons Avignon. This is a beautiful incense perfume favoured by Morrissey and therefore favoured by his fans too. Guillaume has been to 100 Morrissey gigs in 14 different countries: "The gigs are something we can all share. I think Morrissey likes it when he looks at the front row of fans and it's the same people. He recognises us and it's very inspiring. Always we want to be on the front row to share a handshake with him."

Guillaume's girlfriend Ani from Atlanta, Georgia, sports a quiff every bit as good as Morrissey's circa 1992. She is wearing a St Christopher pendant around her neck - the patron saint of safe travel. The couple met outside a Morrissey gig in Prague in 2009. Ani: "Morrissey brings people together".

"How do you get tickets for all these concerts?" I ask: "I had a nightmare trying to get tickets for this tour."

Guillaume: "It's like a military operation. I have to organise my time. I work a lot of weekends to be able to take the time off. When tickets go on sale I take a half day off. I'm like a city trader with several phones in each hand and my computer on. It's like 'Buy! Sell! Hold!'. I can buy tickets for 35 shows in one day. I spend a fortune. But I have to be on the front row at the concert. So if all the standing tickets have sold out I turn to eBay. I was quite glad there were no Morrissey dates in 2010 and so was my bank manager."

I've been in Inverness one hour and still not checked into my place for tonight - the Heathmount Hotel. I run into Mike Wilde, the founder of the legendary 'Quarry Nights' discos which often take place after Morrissey's shows. It's great to see Mike who has been a permanent fixture on the Moz circuit for years. We agree to catch up later.

I walk up a hill to reach the Heathmount which according to its website is "award-winning, independent, small, stylish and friendly," giving guests "a real taste of Inverness." You need to walk through the hotel's restaurant/bar to get to reception. This is my kind of place. The Heathmount only has eight rooms and after climbing a steep staircase I'm in room 7 at the very top. It's lovely, but I'm stressed. It's a familiar feeling. Giddy at being somewhere new but panicky over the most stupid things. Have I got my Morrissey ticket? Have I got my money? Can I plug my iPod into this thing by the bed? Can I stop banging my head on this low ceiling? And I need to shave my head, where's the razor? What do I wear tonight?

Tunes on the go at least - Morrissey's *Vauxhall And I*. After the most clumsy head shave in history I finally make it out onto the streets wearing a 1991 Morrissey teeshirt. Let's get this party started. The nearest pub to the Ironworks, at just three doors down, is the Phoenix. It's 6pm and there's a handful of Morrissey fans inside.

First up, Jamie Skelton from Hull. I'd 'met' Jamie a few weeks ago on Twitter and we'd loosely arranged to meet in Inverness. I'm glad it's happened, as Jamie, 21, seems a top guy who is clearly living the Moz dream. Last night he was in Perth to watch his hero, today he got a new tattoo and now he's ready to rock again. The newly inked word on his right shoulder: *Morrissey*. Jamie: "The tattoo today was spontaneous. I just walked past a tattoo parlour and had it done."

Felton and Skelton sit by the window of the cramped Phoenix. Jamie is chatting at a furious pace. I am too; we're just buzzing at being here. At the bar there is a selection of Black Isle organic beers. The first pint flies down - time for another. We get an even darker looking ale. We don't really enjoy the taste, but none-the-less it storms down. Pint three, another real ale, even darker looking with a slighter better taste. The Smiths are playing on the pub's jukebox.

As me and Jamie discuss our love of Morrissey we become distracted by a hen party of two stood by the bar. We beckon them over. Sisters Jay and Sarah have all the trademarks of a hen party: the Bride-to-be sash, pink hen party rosettes, and the obligatory hen tour teeshirt. But wait, something's amiss. The teeshirt has no mention of an evening with the Chippendales. Instead it details dates with Morrissey. The sisters from Kent join us and start raving about their man. They've seen the singer live "*15 or 16 times*" and travelled to Rome for him in 2006. They have a pet dog called Mr Smith, and once went to Newport Pagnall to "*lose our bags*".

Jay: "The whole hen do has been organised with a Morrissey and Smiths theme. We did a 30 mile cycle ride last week as a tribute to the Smiths *Stop Me...* video."

Sarah: "Through Morrissey we have experienced so many different things. It's the travelling to places you'd never ever thought of visiting that we love. And this time it's like a Morrissey summer holiday."

As the four of us exchange Moz travel stories, it strikes me how wonderful this whole Morrissey thing is. This complete magic of Moz: a group of strangers gathered around a pub table eulogising about a singer and all that comes with him. I've never met Jamie, Jay or Sarah before, but right now it feels like we've known each other for years. Laughs all round, and more beers all round and in about one hour the four of us will be face-to-face with our hero.

We decide it's time. A brief seriousness descends. We drink up and move. A farcical airport-style search operation greets us at the Ironworks. A crack security team frisk everyone. Pockets emptied, coins bouncing off in all directions. It's not ideal. And I can't believe Morrissey would have insisted on this. Is it a legacy of that bottle incident at Liverpool's Echo Arena 18 months ago?

Anyway, we are in. A lovely lady from a local animal rights charity inside the venue is urging Jamie Skelton to go vegetarian. Morrissey invited her to put up her stall in the foyer and fight the good fight. Jamie is all of a fluster with her. Head in hands, the Yorkshireman nods: "I know what you're saying, I'd love to give up meat and be vegetarian like Morrissey but I like my bacon butties too much. But listen, I'll go away and give it some serious thought."

The Ironworks is tiny with a capacity of just 1,000. Jay and Sarah force through to the bar at rear of the dark hall and get some beers in. The four of us then shuffle forward to the left of the stage. It's packed but we have a good position. More familiar faces. Stood directly in front of me: Gary and Alyson Phillips from Aberdeen. I'd first met them at a Moz gig in Glasgow in

2004 and bumped into them at various random music halls across Britain ever since.

I'm nervous. I'm always nervous in the moments before Morrissey comes on stage. I've no idea why the thought sends my head spinning. I've been attending his concerts for 20 years and yet this apprehension before he actually appears remains the same. I felt this way aged 17, I feel this way aged 38. It's just this being face to face with the man who has sung the songs that have been the soundtrack to my life. It's like, any minute, he will be here.

Before Morrissey comes on stage a series of fantastic videos is played. There's Lou Reed and Edith Sitwell interviews, songs from Sparks and New York Dolls. This mixture of music and interview builds the atmosphere and sets the scene superbly.

At 9:10pm-ish the lights dim and suddenly he's here. The crowd surges and a huge roar goes up. I lose Jamie, Jay and Sarah in the frenzy. Morrissey yells: *"Inverness, Inverness, I'm a quivering mess."* First song *I Want The One I Can't Have* followed by *The First Of The Gang To Die*, *Irish Blood English Heart*, *There Is A Light That Never Goes Out*, *Everyday Is Like Sunday*, *Shoplifters of the World Unite And Take Over* and *You Have Killed Me*.

The crowd is hysterical. And I'm speechless. Hit after hit after hit and Morrissey singing every syllable as if his life depends on it. He plays *Meat Is Murder* against a backdrop video of animals getting slaughtered in abattoirs. It's horrendous and graphic. But it has to be done.

Three new songs are aired and sound fantastic. Then even more emotion: I can't believe he goes back to 1986 and sings *I Know It's Over*. I'm swaying and singing and barely believing he is playing this beautiful song. And then during the emotional intensity I remember what Chris Wilde had said about the setlist. I feel for a moment that maybe this could be the end, maybe this is Morrissey saying goodbye and he's going out with a set that is sending the apostles into agony and ecstasy in equal measure.

It's all becoming too much for me. And then a few bars of a song I kind of recognise - a cover of Lou Reed's *Satellite Of Love*. This is Morrissey looking and sounding out of this world. The last song of the night is *One Day Goodbye Will Be Farewell*. All in - 80 minutes, 19 songs, and a feeling of wonderment and confusion for me. It was almost like Morrissey was saying that 'this really is the farewell'. I don't know, maybe those pre-gig real ales have fuelled a Felton delirium. Maybe I'm just reading too much into it all.

Outside the Ironworks, faces are beaming. It has been an amazing Morrissey show. Everyone I come into contact with is raving about the gig. One lad, who introduces himself as Matt, chats about the concert and tells me he's off to Dunoon tomorrow. We're both booked on the 09:18 out of Inverness so agree to look out for each other in the morning.

I walk 200 yards to the Ramada hotel and catch up with Mike Wilde and his pals. We have a pint at the bar. But the conversation is a bit heavy. Morrissey's use of the graphic animal abattoir footage has split opinion. Some fans are all for it, others not. I try to lighten the mood: "But what about the gig? Morrissey was sensational." That's something everyone is in agreement on. A few fans decide to leave, not that they've had enough of the conversation - they are set to drive to Dunoon - right now - at 11pm at night. It will take them three hours at least. And when they reach their destination they're going to sleep in their car. That's crazy. And dedication beyond words. I suddenly feel extremely lucky and privileged to be going to a four star hotel any minute now.

I notice that Morrissey band members Jessie Tobias and Soloman Walker are in the hotel bar a few yards away. Wow, Morrissey must be staying here too. I don't go over. It's been a long day and I'm shattered. So, I say goodbye, get a portion of chips wrapped in the Inverness Courier Newspaper and start the 20 minute hike home.

Interlude 2

"Hi Dickie. I saw you outside the Inverness Ironworks last night, which has led to me dropping you a line.

"On 17th June 1984 I went to see The Smiths at Eden Court, Inverness with my friends. I was 15. As we were settling into our seats, we saw two rather attractive boys. We surmised they were from Charleston (the best local school for attractive boys). Anyway, we were there to witness musical and lyrical perfection, not ogle at boys. Distraction over, we started to concentrate on the gig. Me and my best friend Shona ran down to the very front and I'm ashamed to say we manhandled Morrissey, grabbing at his arms and trying to pull him off the stage. I was totally overawed by the whole experience and was a bubbling snotty wreck.

"Somewhere in the midst of it all, Morrissey took off his pink and white Evans shirt and threw it into the crowd. To our delight one of my mates, Jackie, caught it. We rushed back to our seats but the shirt had disintegrated to a solitary sleeve divided between a pack of hormonal girls. Some other blighter had nicked the rest of our shirt.

"Four years later I met a boy and we got talking. I remembered him from The Smiths concert (he was one of the Charleston boys). We talked about our admiration for all things Morrissey and The Smiths. Anyway, he grabs a book and in between the pages was a massive (A4 size) piece of my shirt. Pink and white in all its glory. My piece of shirt is the size of a book of stamps. Coincidentally, the pieces fitted together.

"I married this boy, not because of the shirt or The Smiths, or because he was called Steven, but for the normal reasons you chose to get married: love, children and all that nonsense.

My piece of shirt, although small, is one of my most prized possessions (next to my children, husband and cats).

"I have given it to my children when they have had exams, when they have sat their driving tests. I have bestowed it with magical luck giving powers. It's a part of our lives, tied up in the mythology of our family. I know that in reality it is just a piece of shirt but it reminds me of my adolescence and my dark, emotional, teenage struggles. It reminds me of one of the best nights I have ever had."

Donna Goodall

...Dunoon

Dunoon

Saturday 18 June 2011,
Queens Hall, Dunoon, Scotland

Saturday 18 June 2011

Up early, ears still ringing from the wall of noise of last night's concert. What a gig, what a night. And today I'll do it all over again. Life's fantastic. I made some top decisions last night. I didn't go on a bender after the gig and I was safely tucked up before midnight. All in, a very respectable start to my Morrissey tour adventure. But hey, there's plenty of time to overdo it. I'm the sole breakfast diner at the Heathmount. Gorgeous selection of fruit followed by poached eggs on toast. It's mostly a silent scene but in the bar tucked away behind the breakfast area there are fellas boozing. It's 8am. I can't work out if they are at the tail-end of a wedding or a wake.

Anyway, I feel top notch this morning. Dunoon, Dunoon, I'm on my way soon. And I'm boosted by unexpected news that my pal Dan Gallagher has decided to make the trip too.

I just received a text out of the blue: "I've been thinking about Dunoon, do you think you can get me a ticket if I take chance and jump on a train from Liverpool? Can I crash in your B&B? yours in Moz, Dan."

We agree to meet in Glasgow Central around lunchtime. Great news but it means I need to trace him a ticket for tonight's show at Dunoon Queens Hall. And with a tiny capacity of 1,000 people it may be a struggle. It's time to make another plea to Chris Wilde and pals to see if they have a spare ticket.

I'm up and out of the Heathmount by 8.30am. Back walking, back moving. I fill my bag with some veggie sandwiches from a super little deli across the road. That's my lunch sorted for later on. I haven't been this sensible on a Morrissey tour for years. In bed early, and making sure I'm keeping myself fed (more of a challenge than you think when you spend entire days sat on public transport).

As I walk back down the hill into Inverness and its cobbled streets I pass a sports shop and gawp at the striking Glasgow Celtic away shirt in the window. It's blindingly bright green and so bad that it's actually good. But why in Inverness have I seen no Inverness Caledonian Thistle shirts?

Inverness looks a lovely place and I'm slightly gutted I didn't spend a bit more time exploring yesterday. No time now, the 09:18 to Glasgow Queen Street waits for no one. Onwards, onwards. I get to the station and stand in a long queue. A handful of Morrissey fans loiter. Once aboard I get to my reserved seat and spot the lad I chatted to last night after the gig.

"Hiya, mate," I say as the train jolts. I might be glad of the company as this leg to Glasgow will take three hours. And so what brings Matt Crist, 34, from Reading to Scotland? While I'm doing just two of Morrissey's Scottish dates Matt is doing four out of the five - on his own - well, until he met me. Matt: "I've been a Morrissey fan for years. I just love the travelling, meeting people and going to places you wouldn't normally visit," he says in his sharp southern accent. "The gigs too, are always great. I've been to around 50 Morrissey concerts in 10 countries around the world. I just love the feeling of being on the road following Morrissey, I just lose track of time and I get lost in the whole experience."

"Have you ever met Morrissey?" I ask. Matt gives a commanding: "No", then a more mellow: "I've just never wanted to meet him. I don't go hanging around the stage door or anything like that. I wouldn't know what to say to him. It would be awful. No, for me it's just the visiting different places that I love most and seeing fantastic concerts at the same time.

"When he announces a tour I just get out my map and see where I fancy going. I've been following Morrissey for 20 years. My first gig was the infamous Finsbury Park Madstock gig when he got coins thrown at him. In the early years I had the odd road trip to see him play in places like Bridlington or Birmingham. But then the day trips turned into overnighters to gigs in Dublin and Paris.

"I just began broadening my horizons and got more adventurous. It's the combining of my love for travelling with my enthusiasm for seeing Morrissey live. Trips to Europe and America were eclipsed by an epic voyage across Scandinavia and into Russia by air. Russia was definitely one of my best experiences following Morrissey."

"Russia? You went to watch Morrissey in Russia? Are you serious?" I can't believe it.

Matt: "Well, I'd always wanted to go to Russia but never had a reason to go. When he announced a gig in St Petersburg I thought 'this is perfect,' I had to go. I flew to Sweden, took an overnight ferry then a series of trains."

"How did you arrange your concert ticket? I'm taking it you're not fluent in Russian..."

Matt: "It was such a difficult concert to plan. Organising the transport and getting the ticket for the gig was a nightmare. No-one spoke English. I had problems even before I set off. For a start I had to get a visa to enter Russia. That was £120 gone immediately. The Russians love their red tape.

"I remember the overnight ferry from Stockholm. There was a band on the ship entertaining passengers. But they kept playing cheesy Michael Jackson medleys and I couldn't understand why. It was only a bit later I discovered that Jackson had died that night. It was surreal.

"Once I entered Russia it was quite frightening. At one point on a train these men in uniforms jumped on and aggressively demanded to see 'my papers'. It was like the KGB or something. They disappeared off with my passport for an age. I thought they were going to kick me out of the country. It was terrifying."

We've been aboard this ScotRail service for 90 minutes but it feels like five. The banter has been great. The only downside is this train has got busier and busier. It's full and it's hot, extremely hot. Like a sweat box. Thankfully there's no KGB-style interrogators demanding to see our papers, just train staff battling with a wonky trolley laden with cold ales. We take the plunge (purely to cool down). Oh, come on, this is a Morrissey tour, it's thirsty work. Sat with our McEwans lager at 11am. Rock 'n' roll.

Freelance journalist Matt doesn't immediately strike me as a Morrissey fan at all. No Moz/Smiths teeshirt, no quiff. He looks more like a football supporter and he is: Manchester United. We shouldn't really be getting on: I'm Liverpool - their arch rivals.

We chat about the desperate state of Premiership football. How the working man has been entirely priced out of the matches. Players' sky-high wages, play acting, the near impossibility of getting tickets to watch the clubs you love. I moan: "I don't watch Liverpool as often as I did. The game is just ruined. It's all about the brand, the money. The real fans are just priced out. It's all about corporate bums in corporate lounges."

"Couldn't agree with you more," nods Matt, "I go to United now but don't even go into the ground. Nowadays I travel to Manchester but when my mates go to see the game I just stay in the pub and watch it on TV. I end up having a better time than they do! Paying £45 for United V Stoke? Nah, I'd rather spend my time and money being sat on a ScotRail train headed to Dunoon to watch Morrissey."

Sipping our lager and staring out at Scotland, two lapsed football fans who get their kicks from gigs not games. Never has the glorious Glasgow fresh air felt so good as when we eventually reach Queen Street. The temperature on the train had been horrendous. It's fantastic to be outside on the streets. We are due to meet Dan across town at Glasgow Central. We walk through the Saturday shoppers and Matt finds a five pound note on the floor. Do you ever get the feeling that your luck is in? We contemplate buying a lottery ticket. I contemplate buying one of those fluorescent Celtic away shirts. I'm getting obsessed. I would never wear it but I need one, I want one.

We enter the rough-looking boozer at Glasgow Central and here's our spur-of-the-moment-man-Dan. Grinning like a Cheshire cat he's sat with lager and luggage. "Dan, this is Matt. I met him on the 09:18 from Inverness. He's a good lad. He likes Morrissey and beer." Within a split second we are laughing, smiling and bubbling with excitement over tonight's date with Moz.

Dan: "It's fantastic to be here. I just really fancied it. The more you talked about Dunoon over the last few weeks the more I wanted to come. Yesterday I just made up my mind. And it's almost exactly 20-years to the day since we both travelled to Aberdeen to see Morrissey for the very first time. Do you remember that? 1991? Staying at your auntie's house?"

We have a pint and Matt considers what time we'd like to get over to Dunoon. Me: "The sooner, the better." We need to catch a 50 minute train to Gourock then take a CalMac ferry for a 25 minute hop across the Holy Loch to Dunoon. It sounds simple but we've got to find a concert ticket for Dan and check into our B&B etc. My usual Morrissey worry starts to creep in as we gaze up from our ale at the train times on the screen above.

Me: "There seems to be plenty of trains going to Gourock, but I'd rather not take any chances and just get over there earlier." Pints supped we emerge into the light. None of us particularly takes the lead in working out the best train to get. Glasgow Central is a huge station, platforms everywhere. It looks complicated but we think we are headed to the right train.

We hop aboard. Then a nervousness. "Are we sure this is the right one?" We ask a shopper who is sat opposite laden with bags. "Och, lads, you don't want this." Wrong train confirmed we dive off and dart to another platform. Another train. This must be for Gourock, surely? We get on, put our feet up, open a can of lager before the train manager announces: "Welcome aboard the 14:25 to Neilston."

Neilston? Oh no - wrong train again. This time the doors start closing and we vault Han Solo-esque as if in the Death Star through swiftly sliding doors. We collapse on the platform laughing. We are a shambles. How can you get on the wrong train twice? Matt: "Dunoon? Jesus, it was easier getting to that Morrissey gig in St Petersburg!"

Eventually we sprint along platforms to get to the correct Dunoon train. Made it, just. It's the sixth choo choo I've been aboard in the last two days and it's brand spanking new. It gleams, it shines, it's spotless. And of course, the bog doesn't work. Matt gets caught short when the toilet door springs open as he's got pants down. The train's ticket collector apologies and bemoans his own employers over the new rolling stock: "Hey, they've spent thousands on these trains lads, and you'd think they'd get the bloody toilet doors to shut properly." I'm now laughing so much my stomach hurts.

We are in buoyant mood when we reach Gourock until we actually step down to the platform. It's absolutely pissing down. It looks like the train station had a roof at some point but it doesn't anymore. It's only a short walk to the ferry terminal. As we queue for the boat my mobile rings and it's a reporter from The Scotsman newspaper asking for my reaction to "Morrissey's controversial comments last night in Inverness".

"Controversial? I don't remember him saying anything controversial." I pass the phone and the buck to Matt who deals with the questioning well. Then I remember Moz had criticised Scottish First Minister Alex Salmond for serving foie gras to dinner guests. (Fois gras is the liver of a goose or duck that has been force-fed). It's coming back to me now, Moz made the comments before playing *Meat Is Murder*.

Crikey, wrong trains, broken toilets, the paparazzi on our trail and now a ship called *MV Saturn* to sail us to Steven Morrissey. *Saturn* is a small ferry which carries a few dozen cars and right now around 50 Morrissey fans. As we stride the gangplank with bags over shoulders it feels like we're embarking on a little invasion. Dunoon, I hope you're ready for the Moz Army. The three of us gather around a tiny table. It's cramped. The lounge area, if you call it a lounge, is rammed with Morrissey fans. One has travelled from Holland. The crossing is too short. I think we'd preferred it longer to take in the scenery. It's beautiful. Hills in the distance, a little mist over the loch, a hint of sun in the distance.

We berth in Dunoon and the first wave of fans swarms onto the wooden pier. Dunoon looks like it may actually consist of just one street. A few hotels, a few pubs, a park opposite the pier and tonight's concert venue is just 50 yards away. A rusting and badly bent bus stop sign points the way to Tourist Information.

We walk over the road to the Queens Hall. It looks like a seen-better-days social club. The outside is adorned with blue tiles, the kind you find in public lavatories. Inside Christmas party lights hang from windows (Christmas was six months ago). "What a venue," I shout giddily. Dan shares my enthusiasm: "I can't believe he is playing a dump like this. It's going to be sensational tonight."

Outside the venue there are bodies in blankets. Fans had driven from Inverness after the Ironworks gig and simply dossed down at the entrance. It's a makeshift cardboard city with the occasional quiff popping out from under the covers. The scene conjures images of an army in the trenches waiting for the command to go over the top. Yet there are still a full five hours before Captain Morrissey takes charge.

Three generations of the McDonald family are here. They've made the relatively short hop from Glasgow. Kathleen, 71, son John, who turns 42 tomorrow, and his daughter Fiona, 12, are making tonight a family affair. John says: "My daughter Fiona had started to listen to Morrissey independently for the last year and it's my birthday this Sunday, so for us Dunoon is the perfect gig. We are so excited. My mum, Kathleen, has been listening to Morrissey for the last 28 years. She wanted to come too and experience the atmosphere for herself."

How wonderful to have three generations of the same family at a Morrissey concert. It's the first time I have seen a 71-year-old Moz fan attending a gig with her 12-year-old Moz fan grandaughter. How fantastic. John: "Mum has always 'got' Morrissey and over the years has asked me to make her compilation tapes, and tonight she'll get to see him for the very first time."

We have 40 lovely minutes chatting to fellow fans outside the venue and I pick up a spare ticket for Dan without much trauma. Superb. Around the back of the venue about a dozen faces, many with American accents, are hanging around waiting for Morrissey to arrive. But we're thirsty. It's late afternoon and we've had a long trek. Cue The Brewery. A pub just yards from the Queens Hall which overlooks the loch and the imposing Argyll Hotel. Black paint, gold letters, The Brewery looks every bit the rough holiday town hostelry. The kind of place you enter with trepidation and a quick exit strategy if your fears are realised.

As it happens there's a chalk board outside leaving us in zero doubt that this is the boozer for us: "MORRISSEY & THE SMITHS PLAYING ON JUKEBOX ALL NIGHT LONG - OPEN TILL 2AM."

The afternoon atmosphere inside is buoyant. There must be 60 people in here - all Morrissey fans, all drinking, all singing. Why can't the local on a Saturday afternoon always be like this? The dying British pub industry would be back on its feet in seconds. Familiar faces everywhere. It's suddenly a reunion of epic proportions. Similar conversations are getting played out all across the bar: "You were at Morrissey's Belfast gig, the Palladium 2006, Ally Pally 92, Leeds 99..." It feels a bit like Christmas Eve minus the crap music.

Hugging, handshakes, camaraderie, bonding, call it what you will, the warmth is amazing. This is what Morrissey 2011 is all about. We quickly get immersed and pints sink in quick succession. It's lovely, it's perfect, it's really time to be finding our B&B.

But we're having too much of a good time to be leaving just yet. I bump into St Helens Morrissey fan Chiko and his wife who introduces herself as Mrs Chiko. I first met the couple outside Morrissey's Llandudno gig in 2006. Mr Chiko has had a few tattoos added since then. His body bears lyrics from the song *First Of The Gang To Die*. Trailing the length of his lower right arm: "*He stole all hearts away*". But that's not enough. Inked across the back of his neck is "*Trouble Loves Me*" - an album track from 1997's Maladjusted.

A moment of realism. Me: "This is great but why don't we find our accommodation, dump our bags and get back here as quickly as we can." I'm sad to be leaving The Brewery. But we do need to get organised. I go into the Argyll Hotel opposite which has a phone line for local cabs. Outside is Margaret Dale who I met last night in Inverness. She's clutching a black book which she has put together herself. The *Word of Morrissey* contains every lyric written by our hero.

"That's fantastic," I tell her with enthusiasm: "As far as I'm aware there is no complete record of Morrissey lyrics anywhere. Certainly not in printed form. But it must have taken you years to pull this together?"

Margaret: "It's taken nine months. And I have spent between six and ten hours every week indexing. When Morrissey releases new material it plays havoc with my indexing system and I have to start all over again. I'm making a handful of copies and I want to give one of them to Morrissey during this tour."

Me: "It's quite a commitment to do something like this and I have to ask, why exactly are you doing it?"

"Because I am lyrics-obsessed. I wanted to have all his lyrics in one place because what I found myself doing was constantly pulling out album sleeves to look at lyrics if a word wasn't clear. There are great online resources but sometimes they take a while to navigate. My idea at first was to have it in a Bible-like format. For me and some other fans I think Morrissey's lyrics are more the word of life for us than the Bible. These are the words we live by."

Me: "I'm gobsmacked. This is just amazing." Margaret lets me leaf through the tome. I feel quite honoured. It's beautiful and it's clear she has put so much of her own life into it.

Margaret: "This book is obviously a very tangible homage to the man. As I started to gather the lyrics in one easily accessible format I started to think about how some topics appeared repeatedly. This led to the idea of sorting out where and how many times words like death, crime and ghosts turned up. That interest led to the index which was the hardest part of the book.

"Haven't you ever thought, wait, in which song does he sing about Pinkie? The index is there to help you out. I found the topic that cropped up most in his songs was love. I also noticed that words like cold and dark came up a lot. And those words were more frequent than *warmth*. The concept of forgiveness didn't appear until *Viva Hate*. And *God* didn't rear his head until *Quarry* I think. So, doing the index gave me an interesting insight into his emotional states..."

It's a fascinating stuff but right now I'd like someone to look up taxi as we need one, urgently. Slight problem, there only seems to be one taxi firm in Dunoon. Not only that, this firm appears to be a one man operation called George. I try the freephone in the reception of the Argyll hotel and feel fortunate when I get directly through to George who tells me he will be along in five minutes.

I have to drag Matt and Dan from The Brewery kicking and screaming to get them inside George's white people carrier. We journey five minutes south to drop Matt off at his B&B. His parting shot, as if he's a sergeant major planning a military operation: "Lads, 40 minutes. Forty minutes and we'll all meet back at The Brewery."

We drive back into Dunoon until we reach 297 Marine Drive: the Ardtully. Oh wow. We pull in off the main road to a huge white house with flowing lawn. It looks splendid. Larger-than-life owner Angela greets us with a lovely smile at the huge front door and shows us to our room which is situated in a side extension with wooden decking. We have a view of the loch.

Angela, dressed in all white, has a look of a loveable hospital matron and she delivers something we aren't expecting: "I wasn't sure who this Morrissey was but then I do remember him from The Smiths. I actually recall seeing The Smiths once."

Me: "What? You've seen The Smiths? Even I didn't manage that."

Angela: "No, no I only saw them on TV. They were at Kew Gardens playing music with school children."

Me: "*Charlie's Bus.*"

Angela: "It was what?"

Me: "*Charlie's Bus* - a kids show from the early 1980s. That must have been on about 1984 - nearly 30 years ago. You've got a good memory. The Smiths and Morrissey went on to a few other things after that..."

Maybe this no internet, no email policy at the Ardtully has left Angela a bit sheltered to the wider world. And to be fair, when you run somewhere as magical as the Ardtully with its views, location and peace, why worry about much else? Our 40 minute downtime is almost up. I stand on the decking outside our room and stare at the tiny boats sailing on the Holy Loch. There is a quiet aura to this place.

White people carrier dead ahead. All hail George, smiling on time. We hop in. "The Brewery please, sir." George: "Och it's really busy down there now." He's not wrong. We arrive to find The Brewery doors shut. It's teatime, three hours from Morrissey time and The Brewery is not letting anyone else in. A takeaway is handily situated next door. So, me and Dan help ourselves to a chippy tea. First rule of Morrissey tour - eat when you get the opportunity. With Matt now reunited with us, we make our way towards the Queens Hall. And exactly like last night there's a long queue and a search operation taking place on entry. I complain to one security person about the unnecessary faff and delay. He replies: "Every venue in Scotland now searches concert goers." I don't believe him and shrug.

Once inside, the Queens Hall actually seems quite spacious. What most thought was the smallest venue on the tour actually feels reasonably big. The three of us venture to the right of the stage, and when Morrissey emerges resplendent in red I lose Dan and Matt.

For the next 80 magnificent minutes it feels like it's just me and Morrissey. I stand surrounded by hundreds but alone. I'm transfixed by the singing, the emotion, the atmosphere. The songs sound amazing. His voice is amazing. *Everyday Is Like Sunday* is amazing, the entire hall sings along as one. Does it get any better than this? Yes - *Satellite Of Love* is the greatest cover I've ever heard Morrissey sing.

As the gig progresses I move over to the left hand side of the stage to watch *I Know It's Over* - one of Morrissey's most moving songs - which nearly has me in tears. Then I move towards the back of the venue and try to take it all in: Dickie in Dunoon watching Morrissey. In a sense I feel like I'm back in 1988 when I first discovered Morrissey during a teenage time of TDK tapes. But this is no nostalgia trip. This is very much the present with a singer in the greatest form of his life.

Afterwards buoyant hordes are outside raving about what they have just seen. American fan Melisser exits the Queens Hall and shows me her Morrissey tattoos. Across her chest are Moz lyrics: "*The sanest days are mad.*" On one arm a London bus with the words: "*There Is A Light That Never Goes Out*". But that's not the full extent of the San Franciscan's Morrissey tattoo tribute. There's another ink that's altogether more hardcore. Melisser leans closer, lifts hands to her mouth and pulls down her bottom lip. Underneath the tattooed letters 'MOZ'. In total Melisser, 30, has eight Morrissey-related tattoos.

The McDonald family are out next. Kathleen has bought a Morrissey teeshirt. The three generations are bouncing with wonderment at a fantastic gig. I find my two men, equally beaming at what they've just experienced. And then it's back into The Brewery. It's packed but we get seats. It's like a league of nations. Sat on one side is Melisser who has joined us, sat the other side is Australian Moz fan, Katrina. Another familiar face John Kier is in the bar too. The Brewery is belting out Morrissey songs. *The Last Of The Famous International Playboys* is aired and as I glance up I notice every single person in here is signing along. A wonderful scene. One I can only recall ever happening with football fans in pubs. This is spontaneous and moving. If only Morrissey could witness this. Does he know that his fans have this good a time when they come to see him?

The notebook that I'm using to take notes on the tour is now being passed around the pub like an autograph book. Melisser writes: "Dunoon: Home of pub singalongs that you wished happen everywhere." Some fans from Ireland are chatting to us, Dan gets the beers in, I get the beers in, Matt gets the beers in, John Kier gets the beers in. The night rolls on and on and on. I notice a side room to The Brewery called The Sound. It's a nightclub playing dance music and the patrons inside look nowhere near as elated as the Moz fans downstairs. Outside The Sound I bump into more Moz fans singing - Mark Sneddon and pals. "How amazing was that gig?" he says to me. "How amazing is this pub?" I reply.

Back downstairs and the bar is about to run dry. Barmaid: "We've sold more ale in one afternoon and evening than we did during the entire Christmas period." More songs, more banter, more slurred conversations among the disciples. Suddenly, it's 2.09am. The hordes stumble dazed into the Dunoon night. Dan: "We need to find another pub or someone who has a hotel with a mini bar..."

"No, Dan. We need to find our beds. Has anyone got that number for George?"

Interlude 3

"I have a tattoo of the letter M on my arm. It's my take on the Morrissey logo. I was stopped in the street in Liverpool last year by a woman...she must have been about 40 something. She grabbed my arm, and said "Excuse me love, is that M for Morrissey?"

I said yes and we had a bit of a talk about him.

"I told her that when people ask what the M stands for I make up a different answer each time. Some people think you are being serious if you say it stands for Morrisons and have an obsession for supermarkets.

"Morrissey to me is just everything. His music is a crutch, an emotional blanket. It's there when nobody else is or when you just need familiar words. The amount of times I have used *Vauxhall And I* to just make everything slightly better is insane.

"The trip to a Morrissey gig in Stirling was just after an awful time in my life. After seeing Morrissey sing the songs that changed my life, I felt this euphoric feeling take over. It was like: Yeah, it's all a bit shit right now, but you're not on your own. His music got me through secondary school, college and university. I got the tattoo as a Christmas present to myself about two years ago."

Olivia Cellamare, 24

York

Saturday 25 June 2011,
Barbican, York, England

Friday 24 June 2011

Any minute now Morrissey will appear at Glastonbury and I'm delirious at the thought, even though I'm 200 miles away in Liverpool.

Me, wife Jen and our two-year-old Frankie have just returned from a five day holiday to Paris. We took the Eurostar from France then a three hour train up from London. Our home is getting a new bathroom put in, so instead of being faced with dust and mess we thought we'd just crash in a nice hotel and extended our holiday by one night at the Hope Street Hotel.

As we settle into a vacation in our own city, I plug my Bose headphones into the huge wall mounted LCD TV. Jen and Frankie sleeping, I dance to Moz once again. It's great, it's wonderful, just dancing to Moz. And it strikes me as the first time I've ever watched a Morrissey gig live on TV.

Saturday 25 June 2011
Barbican, York, England

My biggest worry ahead of tonight's Morrissey's gig at York Barbican is tickets. I don't have a concert ticket and neither does my friend Polly who is making the trip from the north east. When tickets went on sale a few months ago they sold out almost immediately.

Over the last few days one guy on Twitter has been driving a hard and ridiculous non-bargain: "One ticket for tonight's Moz gig...I guess it has to be at least 75 pounds and a copy of your book. Let me know..."

I ain't doing that. I don't quite understand Morrissey fans who try to make a profit out of other Morrissey fans. Tickets for tonight's show are £32.50. When you add on the unfair booking fees/admin fees/just-a-load-of-nonsense fees it comes to almost £40. Twitter man: "Well, with 100 euros...I'm already losing money due to some extra credit card costs etc."

I go back to him: "What if we say £60 and I give you a copy of my Moz book too?! Dickie."
Response: "I booked it via a ticket agency so I paid 100 euros for it. So that's what I want

back for it. Let me know if you're interested. Greetings."

Greetings? Greetings? Is he having a laugh? I'd rather sit outside the Barbican and listen in the street than pay over the odds to be inside. I may be an obsessive Morrissey fan but I'm not stupid. If any fan is thick enough to pay a ton to a legalised touting agency he can't expect someone like me to re-buy it from him for the same fee.

I get to Liverpool Lime Street train station, set for my second consecutive Moz weekend. Tonight I see Morrissey at York Barbican, on Monday it's on to Bradford St George's Hall. I step aboard a lovely modern train headed to Scarborough. York is two hours 14 minutes away. A little jaunt compared to last weekend's journey north. My iPod is shuffling The Sundays *She*, Lambchop *You Masculine You*, The Smiths *What Difference Does It Make?* The Christians *Born Again* and then Wings' *Mull of Kintyre*. Shouldn't I have been playing this song last weekend? And isn't this a song I should be ashamed of liking?

I've not got half as much giddiness as last weekend. I dunno. Is it because I'm headed to York and not some Scottish coastal town I've never heard of? I mean, York is beautiful: cobbled streets, ye olde pubs alongside the River Ouse, Vikings, history, walls, the largest gothic cathedral in northern Europe. Why the apathy?

Maybe because I've been to York stacks of times. It just does not hold any sense of adventure for me. And maybe because the gig is a few hours off and I still need to acquire two tickets. I'm not certain of getting to see Morrissey tonight at all. After last night's fabulous appearance at Glastonbury there may be a few more ticketless fans like me wanting to chance their arm.

I've got great memories of York stretching to my childhood. Day trips visiting the National Railway Museum, weekends crashing at my mate Kev's university halls of residence, a family holiday last year, a great denim shirt bought in the Gap sale. I've been to the York Barbican once before to see James in 1993, supported by the then little-known-band, Radiohead. Whatever happened to them?

The train stops at St Helens and three middle aged fellas get on clutching cans of strong Stella lager. Clad in Adidas, Armani and beer bellies bouncing, the rough-looking trio park themselves right next to me. Suddenly there's a whiff of alcohol and Old Spice aftershave. Their banter is predictably chavvy. I get the impression they are not making their way to York for the gig. One decides to instantly borrow my phone charger to boost the battery on his phone. He isn't the kind of guy I'd say 'no' to.

They ask where I'm going and I reply dismissively: "Oh York, just to see a band."

"Hey, that's a long way to be seeing a band mate. Who is it?" It's a make-or-break moment. Do I lie and just come out with a name of some middle-of-the-road dross they're probably into? Or do I remain true to my convictions and run the risk of getting a load of grief?

Oh sod it: "Morrissey. I'm going to see Morrissey." I know what kind of response I'm likely to get from ordinary boys like these. But instead of the typical snide comments, one replies with: "Oh yes, I've heard he's very good live."

Stunned. Absolutely stunned that a), these guys have actually heard of Morrissey, and b), that they reckon his live act is up to scratch. Anyway, I guess it's time for me to ask a few questions. "Where are you lads off to?" Suddenly they don't want to talk so much. "We are going to pick up a car." I don't offer further questioning.

Anyway, the three seem to be less interested in me and now turn attention to two heavy metal fans opposite. They look suitably different to become the focus. It's typical. Anyone looking remotely at odds with the rest of the train ends up getting hassle. It pisses me off.

If I had a choice I'd rather be dressed like the two Megadeth fans to my right than the scruffy, Stella-swigging, sports gear-wearing clowns I'm currently having to share a table with.

On closer observation, the Megadeth lads are rocking the goth look to the nth degree. Maybe the skull tattoos are a bit much. And the constant discussion about shoot-em-up computer games is insanely boring and somewhat disturbing. The Kalashnikov conversation has not gone unnoticed by Old Spice man, who eyes the Megadeth lads and turns to his pals: "We have two budding serial killers on our hands here."

Train heaves on to Yorkshire. Stalybridge, Marsden, misty moors, rain. This area is one of the most picturesque parts of England. But at the moment it's a bit like a black hole. I haven't had phone or internet reception for the last 20 minutes.

Finally, I get a phone signal, Matt sends a text. He's already arrived in York. He's travelled up by car with his friend, Taylor and they are set to hit the pubs. I don't envy their sleeping accommodation this evening - they have nowhere booked - and are set to kip in Taylor's Honda S2000 sports car post-gig. It's a two seater and Matt is six foot-plus.

Leeds. Sunny Leeds. I lived here for a while. Fantastic gigging city. I saw Morrissey here in 2006 at the town hall for the Ringleaders tour. What a sensational venue, what a top gig. Finally, York. I go to the loo on the far platform to splash water on my face and try to freshen up. Peace is shattered as cleaning ladies dive in and shout: "Everyone out, NOW". I'm frog marched out as iron bars slam down behind me. Nothing like a friendly welcome when you arrive somewhere new.

And so to one of England's most historic cities. Ye Olde York. Not that Californian Morrissey fans, Susan Lew and boyfriend, Miles Brodie, are interested in The Shambles or the 2000-year-old history all around them. They've been camped on concrete outside the Barbican for 20 hours to ensure their place at the front for tonight's gig. It's staggering, but according to the scruffy A4 piece of paper stuck to the venue's front door, Susan and Miles are only seventh and eighth in the queue. I wonder what ungodly hour the likes of Karen, Julian, Margaret, Trinity and Ruth got here yesterday to stake their place?

There are bodies lying under an assortment of sheets and what looks like a set of curtains. Susan and Miles are decked under makeshift bedding sourced from another fan who raided a Dunoon charity shop last weekend. Susan, dressed in a black Smiths *Hatful Of Hollow* sweatshirt has been watching Morrissey live since 1991 but this is her first time in the UK. She says: "I hear York is famous for Vikings and things but the extent of our tourism is just watching the sightseeing bus drive past every few minutes. We won't move from this spot as we want to be as close to Morrissey as we can be. It wouldn't be worth us coming all this way to be stood at the back, miles from the stage."

The couple are set to take in five Moz shows in one week. Miles: "I've seen the setlist and

Morrissey is playing some songs that I've never ever seen him play live."

Me: "I presume you have a hotel but you still preferred to sleep rough? That must have been an ordeal? Miles: "Yes! it was raining and cold. We have a hotel, but we just wanted to be here and in line nice and early." Mind you, the queue holds happy memories for the couple who tell me they first met when Morrissey played San Francisco in 2007.

Some joy on the ticket front as I meet Margaret Gonzalez from Texas; she has a spare. All praise the Lone Star State. "You won't believe how worried I've been trying to get a ticket for this gig," I tell her. "It was one of the first places to sell-out and it's taken right until now to find a ticket." Softly spoken Margaret, 28, is about to deliver more good news: "I think someone over there has a spare ticket too?" It feels like the great escape. Margaret's right - there is another ticket going spare - at face value. What joy. I quickly text Polly: "You will go to the ball!"

Margaret is dressed in a Fred Perry polo. A brand favoured by the disciples ever since Morrissey appeared on the cover of his *Years Of Refusal* album in a blue Fred Perry shirt.

The teacher is in the UK for just three days: "I've seen Morrissey shows in Mexico and the US but never over here. York is really the only gig I could do." Margaret's journey home to Texas will take 21 hours. I want to ask Margaret a bit more about why she's travelled so far for one show but we get interrupted by another fan with floppy quiff who announces: "Morrissey is the reason my marriage failed. My wife said to me 'If you follow Morrissey one more time I will divorce you'. So I told her: 'I fell in love with Morrissey before I fell in love with you'."

Clearly the writing was on the wall for this larger-than-life character whose quiff bounces and sways in the mild York breeze. The fan, who I see at every single Morrissey gig, seems happy to tell his life story but not for his name to go in print or to be photographed. He's travelled from South America for the entire tour and is well used to sleeping outside concert halls in his pursuit of his hero: "For one of the early Morrissey gigs I slept standing up in a telephone box. It wasn't very comfortable as there were three other fans in there with me."

Along with Julia Riley, who runs the True-to-you website, this anonymous Dr Who type character has a stellar number of Morrissey concerts under his belt: "I reckon me and Julia have been to more Morrissey gigs than Morrissey himself," he claims extravagantly. I can't help but challenge him on that: "Oh come off it! You're having me on now!" Fan: "I'm serious. I've been to more Morrissey concerts than Morrissey, if you include some cancelled concerts where we turned up but Morrissey didn't."

After his marriage break-up the fan sold his house and that money has been funding tours ever since. But, the cash is now fast running out: "I have about £1,700 left and when that's gone I don't know what I will do."

This fan is by far the most dedicated I've met so far. But I can't help feel worried. Morrissey being cited as the reason for a break-up? The fan recognises his obsessive Morrissey tendencies can land him in hot water. His girlfriend has already started to voice concerns over his continual absence on the road. His mother thinks Morrissey is some sort of religious cult.

If only everyone was as laid-back as another fan boasting an impressive haircut. Stephen Tait from Edinburgh has a regimented stand-to-attention type quiff. He's catching up on sleep, slouched in the kind of deck chair you plonk in your back garden. I wonder if that was sourced in Dunoon too? I'd like to speak to Stephen, who I saw last weekend in Inverness in his blue denim jacket with photograph of Morrissey circa 1990 on the reverse. But there's no logic in waking a man who is relaxing from the rigours of life on the road.

Anyway, it's time for me to meet up with friends. Tonight I'm staying at the house of a former work colleague. As I walk from the venue I bump into Mike Wilde who is wearing a Sea Shepherd Conservation Society teeshirt. A Morrissey gig isn't a Morrissey gig unless you bump into Mike. A lovely guy, we first met in a pub before Morrissey's gig at Preston Guild Hall seven years ago and got on well ever since. Like me, Mike's carrying bags on his way to his accommodation.

Memories come rushing back as I enter the superb period townhouse owned by another Mike - Mike Queenan. It's three stories high and is just yards from the River Ouse. But it's the proximity to tonight's venue that's the big draw - it's only ten minutes walk away.

It's fantastic to see Mike for the first time in five years. When we worked together in Leeds we'd sometimes catch gigs together. Actually, it was only Morrissey and Wedding Present concerts we ever went to. Mike introduced me to the boy, Gedge, and I'd got into them in a big way. As we reminisce over a cup of tea, Mike introduces me to his girlfriend, Aileen, and then Polly arrives. It's like a reunion. I haven't seen Polly since my wedding day in 2008.

It's time to get this party started but I'm dressed like I should be at a funeral. Black shirt, black tuxedo, black tie with Morrissey's face on it lending a glimmer of light to my look. I think I'm just keen to smarten up since last weekend, when it was jeans, tees and Converse.

If I hadn't been chomping at the bit for this gig before, I am now. The four of us walk up to Mike's local The Fulford Arms. It's empty until Matt arrives with his pal, Taylor. Real ales all round, the girl behind the bar plays The Smiths for us.

From the outside York Barbican resembles a League One football stadium. It's all brick, glass and modernity; a contemporary contrast to the Ironworks and the Queens Hall. The venue has just undergone a £2m redevelopment and it shows. "Welcome to the York Barbican, sir," says the smartly dressed attendant as we waltz through the foyer. "Have a lovely evening". Can you believe this? No bag search, no frisking, no security staff feeling my buttocks. All hail customer service and sense of warmth at this fine venue. It couldn't have been a more different welcome at the venues in Inverness and Dunoon last week. There's an altogether more relaxed feel to the Barbican. Good job I'm wearing my tuxedo.

Once done with the pleasantries, the atmosphere in the auditorium is electric. The crowd inside is crazy. Morrissey enters with a Yorkshire phrase - *Ee bar gum* - and the crowd goes mental. First song in this pressure cooker atmosphere - *I Want The One I Can't Have* - and the roar is unbelievable. The *Grand Old Duke of York* is dressed in white shirt and jacket; I knew it was a good idea to go more formal tonight.

Next song *First Of The Gang To Die*, and the Barbican goes berserk. The crowd up front is swaying and jumping up and down. We're dancing too, but are just a bit further away from the madness. It's just fantastic. Matt can take no more loitering and wades frontwards, eager to get a handshake from Moz.

You Have Killed Me, *Shoplifters*, *The Kid's A Looker*, *Ouija Board Ouija Board*, and then *There Is A Light That Never Goes Out* all follow. We dance, sing, sway and just marvel at what amazing form Morrissey is in. He is quite simply unstoppable when he is this good.

And then a smashed glass and my attention diverts left and away from the stage - a punch-up in full swing among the audience as Morrissey sings: "...to die by your side..." It looks a bit tasty and there is zero security anywhere to sort things out. It's hardly *Murder On The Dancefloor*, it's just two idiots slugging it out. But it drags on and it's not that far away from me. An air of menace that I didn't expect at a Moz show.

Order restored, the rest of the set is a joy to witness. My highlight again, the ever wonderful, beautiful, powerful, emotional Lou Reed cover, *Satellite Of Love*. It seems that all 1,800 of us sing as one.

A huge football crowd-style chant of "Morr-iss-ey, Morr-iss-ey" reverberates around the Barbican as our hero enters for the encore. *This Charming Man* plays out to scenes of fans desperately trying to get on to the stage. As the crowd bays for more, Morrissey is gone and the rest of the band walk off applauding the crowd. Awesome, absolutely awesome.

Outside, the atmosphere bubbles. Croaky voices, fans wet with sweat and beer, dishevelled teeshirts. Everyone has a smile and everyone wants more Moz. We dive into the Phoenix Inn - which is actually pretty similar to the Phoenix pub in Inverness. Sat outside is Shed Seven frontman, Rick Witter.

Six of us go for a curry, which is a great way to wind down after what has been a fantastic day. As veggie korma is consumed a huge debate gets underway about The Smiths potentially reforming. Mike urges: "They have to. It would be amazing. Morrissey and Marr back together again." Me and Matt fight for things to stay exactly as they are. Matt: "If The Smiths reformed it would be awful. I wouldn't even go and see them. The Smiths is dead. Morrissey is the here and now." Hear, hear.

Anyway, Matt doesn't want to disagree with Mike too much as he's just offered him and Taylor his floor for the night. Which is a damn sight better place to sleep than Taylor's Honda.

Sunday 26 June 2011

I say goodbye to Matt. He's not doing the Bradford gig on Monday. Next weekend he's off to see Morrissey for two nights in Krakow and Warsaw. Mike drops me back at York train station in his red sports car. The girl serving me a cup of tea looks unimpressed when I tell her I'd been to see Morrissey and that I was now on my way home. Well, it was her that asked.

"Morrissey who?"

"He's a bit like Elvis Presley."

"Oh right. My mum would probably like him."

As I loiter and consider which train I'm actually going to get today, I notice three Morrissey fans clad in teeshirts and carrying bags. "What a gig," I say. "Amazing," the three say in unison. These are not English accents. Renata Spinola and husband, Arthur, have flown in from Brazil. They are with their friend, Luciana, who lives in Manchester.

Renata: "Last night was my first ever Morrissey concert. It has been a dream of mine to see him live but we don't get very many opportunities to see him in Brazil. We started queuing at 2pm and got a spot on the second row, central part of the stage. I was so happy. But before he started the first song I was getting squashed and got pushed back."

"Yeah, I thought it was a pretty rough crowd last night," I say. "I mean, it was a great atmosphere, but very rough too."

Renata: "One woman near me fainted and I saw two fights. But I'd read how crazy people can be at his English shows. I cried twice last night. Once because I lost my spot in front of him and then later on because I was finally at one of his concerts. It's like my dream had come true."

Me: "The fights were completely out of character for a Morrissey gig. I can honestly say in 20 years of going to his concerts, the fight last night was the first I'd seen."

Renata, a university professor, is seeing Morrissey twice more this week, in Grimsby and Plymouth. "A week of Moz hey, it doesn't get much better than that," I say.

Renata: "I've been a fan since I was 12. Morrissey has been part of my life for so long that I cannot think of myself without thinking about him. All my life has been guided by him. I spent my adolescence listening to his songs and trying to figure them out. I couldn't understand a word in English but I was sure those songs were trying to tell me something. There were something special about them. I started to study English by myself because I desperately needed to understand his message.

"I didn't need too much time to fall in love with him. Those lyrics were sensational and they really said something about my life. I felt like someone was writing those things specially for me. I grew up listening to Morrissey and I always turn to him and his lyrics whenever I need comfort, hope, help, when I'm happy, sad, when I need a friend, when I'm in trouble."

Me: "I think a lot of us feel the same way. And that's why we go and see him so many times. Like he's been a major part of our lives and continues to be."

Interlude 4

Email Sunday 26 June 2011

"Hello Dickie,

"We are Giovanni and Daniela from Italy and we want to tell you our story. We love Morrissey since 1984 but the first time we met was in London, Wembley Arena, December 8th 2006.

"I (Giovanni) started from Sardinia (my country) and Daniela from Venice to see the Man.

"It was love at first sight... because from that day we are inseparable and in May 2009 we married. *Sweetie Pie* was the soundtrack during the wedding.

"We planned our honeymoon following the 2009 European Moz tour, so by car we went from Venice to Paris (aargh the concert was cancelled, also the Lille concert was cancelled) and so we went to Luxembourg to finally see Him.

"One month later we went to Wien by car and in this occasion I gave Morrissey a Pasolini photographic book and I can't forget his smile and his "Grazie". In the same year we took the car again and we drove up in Munich, this time I gave Him an old Gigliola Cinquetti vinyl and we touched His hand. What a special moment, REALLY!

"So, Dickie this was to tell you that Morrissey changed our lives not once but twice: when we first listened to him and the second when he brought us together.

"So politely, Giovanni and Daniela."

Bradford

Monday 27 June 2011,
St George's Hall, Bradford,
England

Monday 27 June 2011

I'd left York yesterday and travelled north. Jen and Frankie were up in Penrith, Cumbria, staying with family. None of us particularly wanted to be at our home in Liverpool while our old bathroom was getting ripped out and a new one put in. So I joined them and spent yesterday larking around with Frankie and taught him to sing Satellite Of Love.

Tonight will be my fourth Morrissey gig in nine days. I get to Penrith station mid morning to board a train south. The Pendolino is late and the station announcer keeps going on about *"gold zone, purple zone, standard class, first class, stand here, stand there"*. Am I finally getting bored of rail travel?

This is the first train of the tour that's late. By six minutes. I can't complain about the rail network at all in terms of punctuality. But I can moan about the fact it's expensive and almost every single train I've used has been packed.

I get on, it heaves on to Preston. No seats anywhere. And so I stand. This is going to be a long day. Tonight Morrissey plays Bradford St George's Hall. I need to get back to Liverpool, check on the bathroom, then get my car, pick up Dan and head to West Yorkshire. We need to return immediately after the gig as we're both back in work tomorrow. All-in-all it's packing in a lot and I'm not entirely sure I have the energy.

As my train travels through the Lake District I reminisce about the times I've seen Morrissey play at St George's Hall. Tonight will be the third time I've seen him appear in the West Yorkshire city.

In February 1995 Morrissey was supported by Marion. Me and my university chums met Marion the afternoon of the gig. I can't believe my memory stretches 16 years but I recall bumping into the band at Bradford Interchange train station. They were in the newsagent and signed a diary I used to carry with me everywhere. I've still got the diary.

I watched Morrissey in Bradford again in 2002 supported by Sack. That gig of nine years ago was one of my most memorable ever Morrissey gigs. During the set we unfurled our Liverpool FC flag which has the words: *"There Is A Light That Never Goes Out"*. Morrissey spotted it and said: "Is it the Bootle Bruisers? Is it? I always get this wrong. Is it Dickie and his friends?" I'm not sure how he knew my name. We'd taken the flag to two Morrissey shows six weeks earlier at The Royal Albert Hall and been photographed by Linder - a close friend of Moz. Maybe Linder had told him about the banner? We were ecstatic that Morrissey had mentioned us.

The reason I remember those support acts is that they were so good. Apart from a few minutes in Inverness last weekend I haven't seen any of the support acts on this tour so far. Shame on me, because the support act is a vital ingredient to the whole Morrissey live experience. It stands to reason, but the more you follow a Moz tour, the more you enjoy the support. Over three or four nights on the road you get used to the songs, the sound, the words. There are some Sack songs today that mean as much to me as Morrissey songs.

He's always taken amazing groups or singers on the road with him. In 2009 it was Doll and the Kicks who were absolutely superb. The singer Hannah always hung around after the Kicks' set to chat to fans.

Train stops at Oxenholme, Lake District. On the platform there are people everywhere, rushing around, lugging huge cases. The Oxenholme public address man directs people to another platform with some very frank advice: "The Leeds train goes from platform one, and if you want to make it in time don't even think about using the lift." So anyone with a pram, wheelchair, or heavy case has zero chance of making that one then.

And that's what's wrong with rail travel in Britain. I hate driving and motorway travel in particular. Given the choice I'd choose rail travel every single time. But you get the impression that to the rail industry us passengers are just an inconvenience. We are customers paying over the odds for the privilege of overcrowded trains and station lifts that don't work. I couldn't even wash my face at York train station on Saturday without being made to feel like an inmate at Strangeways.

I get home. The house is a wreck. Dust everywhere and the bathroom in a state of disrepair. That restroom at York would be more use right now. And so I check myself into Crosby Lakeside Lodge, which is actually a sports centre but does a cracking sideline in cheap but super spacious rooms. I'm weary; this will be the eighth different bed I've slept in in the last 10 days.

I check in to the Lakeside and aim to leave for Bradford in ten minutes flat. It's mid afternoon. I grab my car keys, bottle of water, packet of Polo mints (vegetarian) and concert ticket. I fill up at Shell Waterloo. It costs £35 to half-fill the tank. I get to Dan's place. He's again making the trip ticketless. We hope to get him his pass to paradise outside the venue. I'm ok for tonight; a fan up in Inverness had a Bradford ticket going spare.

Driving, the whole concept of driving in Britain appalls me. We hit the M62. Everything is slow for a while until we get near West Yorkshire when we grind to an absolute halt. And then one hour turns into two hours. Stuck on some bland inner ring road in the queue of all queues. It's not like there has been an accident up ahead; this street stalemate is probably entirely normal for teatime on a chronic Monday. And that's where the problem lies. Too many cars, too much traffic, not enough road. We've become a country of two-car families who drive here, there, nowhere.

I once had a job that involved lots of driving. Hated it. Other than listening to tapes from the 1980's, there's nothing productive about spending four hours each day stuck in a traffic queue. Bad for body, madness for your mind. I left. I got a job closer to home and now take the bus to work.

Funnily enough I had also driven to Bradford for that Moz gig in 2002 and returning in the early hours got a speeding ticket. My first and last speeding ticket. I was caught doing 59mph in a 50mph zone on an empty motorway slip road at 1am. Hardly *Boy Racer* material but enough for a £60 fine and three points on my licence. I think my downer on driving started that very night.

It's now 6pm and we are only seven miles from Bradford. But we may as well be 70 miles away. The only thing that is keeping me from abandoning my vehicle REM-*Everybody Hurts*-style is the company. Good ole Danny G. His spur of the moment Dunoon dash was such fun, he's decided to give it another go.

And so on this bleak concrete crawl we reminisce about past Morrissey trips. Dan was my active Moz gigging partner between 1991-1995. We both witnessed Morrissey's first solo tour and went to gigs in Aberdeen, Liverpool and Blackburn that spring/summer. Those three nights were the very start of our journey.

Dan was the only lad at my school who shared my love of Morrissey. I remember the excitement we'd have on the day of a new release. In 1992 we both bought *Your Arsenal* on vinyl and gave it a first airing in the bedroom of his Formby home over a few cans. This was pre-internet days when you'd buy a record and have little idea what wonders it had in store for you until *needle hit groove*.

Two decades on and we park up in Bradford. A short walk to St George's Hall and the real work starts as we try to source a ticket for Dan. I trail the length of the queue and again it's full of familiar faces. But the familiar luck with tickets is absent. Dan tries the Queen pub, which is bursting full of Morrissey fans but none with a spare. "This may not be our night," I sigh: "But let's keep trying."

There's a great buzz outside the venue. The weather is nice. Boz Boorer makes an appearance and shares photographs and banter with fans. "I wonder if Boz has a spare ticket?" cracks Dan. It's not a bad suggestion but we can't go asking tickets from the group. Can we? We don't, because a fan with close links to Morrissey's tour crew tells us he can help us out. "Just hang on here and I'll see what I can do." And so we hang on like little lost sheep. "This is doing my head in, Dan, hanging around in the hope this guy is going to box us off with a ticket."

We persevere and our well-connected fan suddenly appears with a member of the Morrissey team who is taking a handful of returns back to the box office. We hang in suspense inside the box office until the fan offers Dan a seat at face value. He's in. Panic over we celebrate with a portion of chips and a hot cup of tea in the hottest chippy ever. Sweat literally pours off brows in the window seat, getting a tan in sunny balmy Bradford.

Bradford is probably most famous for its part in the industrial revolution. The old cotton mills are still here, but these days transformed into swanky apartments. The city was used as the location for much of the 1963 movie, *Billy Liar*. Many of the Victorian buildings and streets featured in the film are still around. Today, Bradford has fantastic Indian restaurants and a National Media Museum. I'm not sure whether my once favourite building here - the city library - has survived all this regeneration. That place holds a very special place in my heart. Nearly 20 years ago I found a copy of Morrissey's 1983 book *James Dean Is Not Dead* and borrowed it for a few weeks. Copies of the tome, written by the singer before he hit the big time, now sell for £200 on eBay.

The city centre may have changed these days, but some of the old pubs remain. We sample a few. I push the boat out with several blackcurrant and sodas. Dan gets on the ale. We bump into a few people who were up in Dunoon - a gig and night which have now taken on mythical status among everyone who was there.

As we get to the grand, imposing, historic St George's Hall, it's time to temporarily say goodbye. Dan is up in the seats while I'm down in the standing. I'd forgotten what a maze this theatre is. For the lower standing section you seem to scale stairways upwards rather than downwards. A search, a frisking, but not as intense as Scotland.

I catch the last few videos before Morrissey comes on stage. There is literally no room to be had anywhere. It is absolutely packed and the atmosphere is electric. Oh my God, second song is *You're The One For Me Fatty*. One of his greatest ever singles and I can't believe I'm here to witness him singing it. It's been 20 years since I witnessed *Fatty* live - I think Manchester Apollo,1992.

The crowd goes crazy. But rather than gaze at the stage my eyes are pulled high right to the seats which run around the venue. There's fan Stephen Tait, in his magnificent quiff singing his heart out from the balcony. He looks like Morrissey, he moves like Morrissey. The night gets better and better with more-or-less the same set from Saturday at York. I'm finding my familiar calling towards the rear of the venue. Morrissey is very chatty. He mentions York and says he was bored visiting the Minster. Morrissey is absolutely on fire. *I Know It's Over* is a few moments of misery and majesty. And everybody, absolutely everybody, sings and feels each and every line. It's emotion, it's devotion, it's all over too soon.

Outside in the now chilly Bradford air, Dan hands me an orange juice. "Jesus, it looked crazy downstairs on the floor. You must be thirsty? What a gig. What a gig. An absolute sensation."

We walk to the side of St George's to see a car and around 100 fans, waiting for Morrissey. Crowd barriers laid out, security staff look nervous, fans clutch Sharpies in hope of their moment. Then he appears from the darkness, resplendent in light jacket and jeans. He glides past everyone, dives into the backseat and his car screeches off.

Interlude 5

Email June 2011

"Dear Dickie, I had front row tickets to see Morrissey at the Liverpool Empire - my mum actually queued up for the tickets. She bought front row, how magical? During the song *Let Me Kiss You* Morrissey ripped his shirt open and threw it to the crowd. Dickie, I LEAPT and I caught the shirt. I curled myself into a ball as the claws around me scraped my hair, scratched my ears and neck.

"I didn't care, the pain was worth it, he is worth it. So, I stuffed the shirt into my trousers - where else would it go, Dickie? I then stood up as many applauded my treasure. I realised his shirt had touched his skin, his heart pouch - it was intact - the full shirt - now my shirt.

"Before the encore, I ran and ran, I jumped into a pub off the beaten track, I took out the shirt, slowly - these things take time, Dickie - I could not believe my eyes, the night had opened my eyes, it was Morrissey's shirt, it smelt beautiful, it was my cape, my mate, my fate. After texting anyone who knows me, whether they wanted to hear it or not, I told the world. I phoned my mum - she phoned my dad - he was on nights, it made his night - a shirt made our night, my night, day, year, life.

"I took the shirt home and placed it on a hanger (after trying it on, well I had to, posed for the camera too), I took the arm of the shirt and placed it under my pillow.

"As I lay on the pillow, I awoke at 5am and saw the shirt and just thought, Morrissey smells lovely. The shirt is the only item of clothing I like."

Matt Jacobson, 38, Aigburth, Liverpool

Isle of Man

Monday 1 August 2011,
Douglas Villa Marina, Isle of Man

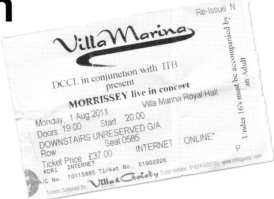

Sunday 31 July 2011

"Oh come on, Dan. You know you want to," urges Matt over a few pints at Crosby's Crows Nest pub. Tomorrow we catch a ferry to the Isle of Man for Morrissey's gig at the Villa Marina. From our vantage point in the Crows' beer garden tomorrow's trip looks all plain sailing but Danny G remains docked due to work commitments.

There's four of us going tomorrow. Me, Matt, and my pals Latta and McCully who put together sound like some sort of 80s detective duo. I've been going to gigs with Latta for nearly two decades, watching Morrissey everywhere from Preston to Paris. We've been so much a fixture on the Moz circuit that if one of us was at a gig and the other wasn't it would raise eyebrows: "Where's your partner in crime?"

The first Moz gig I attended with McCully was Chester Northgate Arena in 1997. A sensational afternoon was spent sampling the pubs of Olde Deva before watching Morrissey in a tiny sports hall. One of the best gigs of my life.

Monday 1 August 2011
Douglas Villa Marina, Isle of Man

As soon as Morrissey announced a gig in the capital, Douglas, we were onto it immediately. Sun, sea, songs, on an island situated in the middle of the Irish Sea. The Isle of Man is around 80 miles from Liverpool and for us at least, easy to get to with a daily ferry. The Isle of Man is self governing with a population of just 85,000. The island is 32 miles long and just 14 miles wide. It's tiny and it's amazing that Morrissey is visiting.

Like Dunoon, Douglas is not the usual destination on a tour trail. The only artists to have visited in recent years include Will Young and Status Quo. So there is much excitement at the first proper singer coming to town.

Isle of Man has its own parliament and Morrissey's visit even has politicians giving the right kind of spin. Last month the Community, Culture and Leisure Minister David Cretney

INVERNESS

MORRISSEY & THE SMITHS PLAYING ON JUKEBOX ALL NIGHT LONG

OPEN 'TIL 2am

DUNOON

D U N O O N

TICKET NUMBER : GA4 25
UNRESERVED

ticketmaster
ticketmaster.co.uk

DF CONCERTS PRESENT
MORRISSEY
QUEEN'S HALL, DUNOON
UNDER 18S PERMITTED
DOORS 7.30PM
SATURDAY 18TH JUNE 2011
PRICE 22.50 S/C 4.75 TOTAL 27.25

MORRISSEY QUEUE

1. MAREN
2. Julian
3. Margaret
4. Huw
5. Trinity
6. Ruth
7. SUSMO2
8. MILES
9. VIVIAN
10. GLORIA
11. Christine
12. Lottie
13. Lucy
14. John
15. DEMOTHY
16. Guillaume M—
17. ANI SMITOXX—
18. LOR
19. Nathalie
20. Chayane—

21. Jenna
22. Margaret
23. STEPHEN
24. RUTH
25. Manuel
26. CAROL
29. Jack H
28. Curtis B
30. AYAKO
31. GRILL
32. Kathrine
33. Steph
33. JESSICA
GEORGIA
Thomas Haupt
Deborah.
Annelie Boettger
Julian (Samuel
Roy
40. GREG
41. LUCIANA KAROES
42. RENATA SPINOLA
43. ARTHUR CARIA FILHO
44. Maria Chadwic

YORK & BRADFORD

STANDING

MORRISSEY
AFTER-SHOW DISCO
Monday JUNE 27th

RIO'S BRADFORD
5-7 Barry Street, Bradford

ISLE OF MAN

THERE IS A LIGHT
THAT NEVER GOES OUT

1ST AUGUST 2011

ROYAL HALL

MORRISSEY

Villa Marina   Re-issue N

DCCL in conjunction with ITB
present
MORRISSEY live in concert
Monday, 1 Aug 2011   Villa Marina Royal Hall
Doors 19:00   Start 20:00
DOWNSTAIRS UNRESERVED G/A
Row   Seat 0585
Ticket Price £37.00
KCR.1   INTERNET   INTERNET   ONLINE*
A/C No. 1011586S Ticket No. 01902226
Tickets Supplied by: Villa & Gaiety Ticket Hotline 01924 680555 www.villagaiety.com   P

Under 16's must be accompanied by an Adult

WEST
INTERSTATE
10

EVENT CODE
SM1114
$ 55.00
$ 12.75
SECTION/AISLE
OR RC
VI 17X
ROW SEAT
Z 106
MJT1156
A14NOV

SECTION/AISLE   ROW/BOX SEAT   ADMISSION
OR RC   Z 106   ADULT
USE ORCH AISLE 3   55.00
C3 PRESENTS
MORRISSEY
SPEC GUEST KRISTEEN YOUNG
MAJESTIC THEATRE
SAN ANTONIO, TEXAS
MON NOV 14 2011 7:30PM

EVENT CODE
ESM1114

2-39903
SEC   OR RC
VI507MJT
ROW   SEAT
A   55.00
SEAT
106

ticketmaster
BUY TICKETS AT TICKETMASTER.COM

72270916305

CINEMA   PM 15

HISTORIC
H
O
U
S
T
O
N

MORRISSEY

SAN ANTONIO

AUSTIN

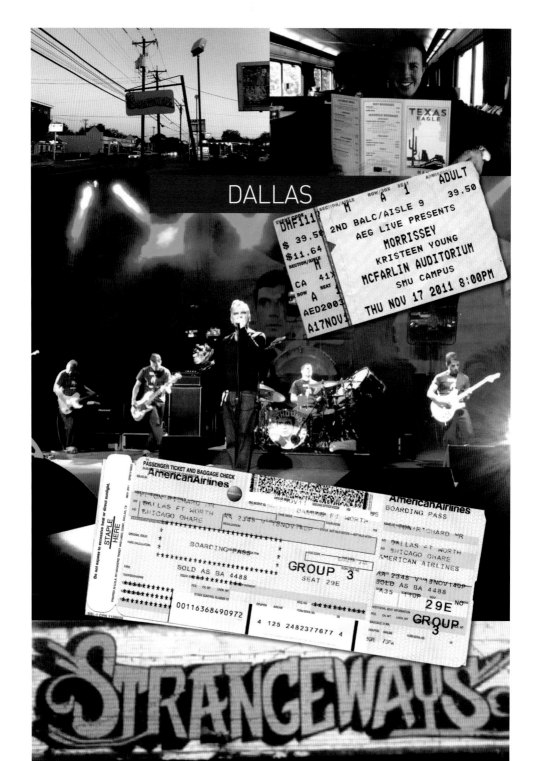

DALLAS

EVENT CODE   SECTION/AISLE   ROW/BOX   SEAT
DMFI11...   M   A   1   ADULT
$ 39.50   2ND BALC/AISLE 9   39.50
SECTION/AISLE   AEG LIVE PRESENTS
$11.64   M   MORRISSEY
CA   41X   KRISTEEN YOUNG
ROW   SEAT   MCFARLIN AUDITORIUM
A   SMU CAMPUS
AED2003   THU NOV 17 2011 8:00PM
A17NOV1

ROME

MANCHESTER

MCR
arena
mcr-arena.com

MHK told media: "I know that this has been a highly anticipated announcement in recent weeks and I am delighted to be able to confirm that Morrissey will be coming to the Villa Marina."

Matt stopped at my house last night. It would have been pushing it to drive up from his home in Reading for today's 11:15am sailing. We catch the train into Liverpool city centre and settle down to breakfast at Moose which does fabulous authentic American and Canadian breakfasts. Is it too early for huge hot waffles served with maple syrup and ice cream? Of course not, we've a Morrissey concert to go to.

As we tuck in, our St Helens sleuths Latta and McCully turn up. Hugs and handshakes all round. "Lads, let me introduce you to Matt. I picked him up in Inverness the other month."

I'm running out of words to describe the excitement we feel. The anticipation, the eagerness, the enthusiasm, the thrill. Morrissey tonight in Douglas, Isle of Man. I know I'm going to enjoy every single moment of this trip. Waffles all round.

The ferry will be leaving from Pier Head which boasts one of the greatest skylines in the world. Liverpool looks amazing from here. The Liver Building - Grade 1 listed - is home to the mythical Liver Birds at the very top which are the symbol of this great city. The Liver Building is accompanied by the Cunard Building and Port of Liverpool Building. They are collectively known as *The Three Graces*. Last week a new £72m Museum of Liverpool was opened nearby. So now the modern meets the historic.

This is a Unesco World Heritage Site and is home for me. So it's with a sense of pride we start our journey from this very spot. Even Matt, from down south, is taken with this fabulous location: "You know I've always liked Liverpool," he insists as the four of us survey the scene. "I can't believe all the new building work that has gone on in recent years. It really complements the existing environment."

As Matt begins to sound like a tour guide, it's time to get aboard our vessel. I'm probably doing *Manannan* a disservice by describing her as a ferry. She is actually a sleek, modern catamaran, her name not to be confused with that of former Liverpool FC attacking midfielder, Steve McManaman.

As we shuffle along in a queue at the ferry terminal, Latta is weighed down by a bag full of lager: "Lads! I'm not paying on-board prices for the ale! It's a recession, we've got to watch what we spend, it's all about beating the system and not giving money to *The Man*." Latta has even brought plastic pint glasses. This he hopes, will enable us to pour our own ale while making it look like we've bought them from the bar aboard. I sense that within minutes of us getting aboard cans will be opened. And there is much to celebrate; McCully is 40 years-young today. What a lovely way to spend such a milestone: a gentle cruise across the Irish Sea for a date with Morrissey.

We sit in the bar of *Manannan*. It is the largest vessel of its kind to sail the Irish Sea. It will take two hours 45 minutes to sail into Douglas. Before we embark the captain gives us a potted history of his vessel and its intriguing name; *Manannan* being the celtic name for God of the Sea.

There's been such a feel-good factor about this trip which started the moment we booked the concert tickets from the Villa Marina. We discuss the fact that there were no booking or admin fees added on. That's right: nothing, zero, gratis. So a £37 ticket remained at £37 with no rip-off extras.

As *Manannan* shifts into gear, Latta carefully but quickly dispenses his first can into a pint glass and observes: "So, what is the Villa Marina getting right that ticket outlets can't get right over here? I was amazed there was no booking fee. Fantastic. It puts you in a good mood from the off." We are in giddy spirits. Spice Girls and S Club 7 play on TV screens as we head towards the misty open sea. On seeing Latta's success, we all discreetly pour cans of ale into our plastic pint pots. Feet up, away we go.

In the four-seater behind us are three fellow Morrissey fans. Gemma and Debbie are with a younger lad, Curtis. I recognise Gemma's face from various gigs over the years but this is the first time we've had a conversation. The three are as buoyant as we are about tonight's show. They have a copy of Chat magazine which by some strange coincidence has an article entitled: "Isle of Man Spooky Special".

Debbie who lives in Washington, Tyne and Wear, tells me how she was looking for a ticket for the Bradford gig in June and Curtis had a spare. When they met up at St George's Hall they went out afterwards and bumped into Gemma. So the three friends, who look like they have known each other years, have actually only been acquainted for six weeks. The power of Morrissey now sees them sailing the seas together

Debbie: "We'd all met for the first time at the Bradford gig. A few weeks later, after too many drinks, we were all chatting on Facebook and all decided we were going to do Douglas. I became the travel agent and have booked us into a four star apartment. And here we are."

Debbie: "We hardly know each other. But that's the nice thing about Morrissey fans don't you think? We're kind of like one big family. So you're never actually alone at a gig. There's always someone to travel with or share a hotel."

Curtis, from Manchester is excitedly bouncing around *Manannan* trying to organise trips to even more Morrissey gigs. After tonight Morrissey plays Belgium on Thursday then Holland on Friday. Curtis: "Who is coming to the shows later in the week? I've priced it up. I think it's do-able. Who else wants to come?"

I speak to a fan who is travelling on her own. For Rowena George, this is not just another jaunt to see her hero. This journey is symbolic. She is going through a marriage break-up and is coping with the recent loss of a fellow Moz devotee.

"I'm here in memory of my friend Darren Connor from Carlisle who died suddenly just a few days after he went to the Dunoon gig. He was just 40 and had a heart attack. He was a huge Morrissey fan. Darren saw Morrissey for the first time when he was just 11. He used to tell me a story of seeing Morrissey going up the escalator in Binns department store in Carlisle when he was appearing at the Sands Centre. I've been devastated by Darren's death. One night I wondered whether there was any Isle of Man tickets left and I just sat up late booking the ferry and a guesthouse. I'm doing this trip in Darren's memory. I thought it would be an adventure and I'd meet some new people. And I'm looking to Morrissey to help give me a new start and confidence to move on with my life after all that's happened."

I'm stunned by Rowena's story and I entirely understand her wanting to follow Morrissey in memory of Darren. I hope this gig can help in some small way. It's not too long before we've crossed our *Moon River* and arrive at the Isle of Man. Matt jokes: "Ok guys, we are now entering the Isle of Man. It's time to set your clocks back 20 years." We drag our bags along the promenade, Douglas is busy with holidaymakers and so it should be; this is the height of the summer season. The coastal town has scores of guesthouses lining its seafront. Horse-drawn trams parade up and down, children play in the sun. It's a bit like Dunoon but bigger, busier and sunnier.

It's mid afternoon and hot. As we reach the Villa Marina venue I spot fan, Stephen Tait, and pals enjoying an ice cream in the gardens. Palm trees and Stephen's quiff sway in the mild breeze. It looks like a lovely way to spend a Monday afternoon. The only strenuous activity seems to be a sporadic football kickabout. You know, this whole Morrissey tour feels like one big holiday. Sun, sea, sundaes, soccer. Where's Morrissey? I reckon he'd join in an impromptu game of five-a-side.

What a marvellous place is the Villa Marina. It's like a huge mansion set in lavish gardens. It reminds me of the beautiful Hotel Del Coronado in San Diego. We bump into Chris Wilde, who looks a little worse for wear. He arrived yesterday and spent last night sampling the Douglas nightlife with some of the other *Irregular Regulars*. No such over exertions planned tonight though; Chris is on the first plane out and straight into work tomorrow morning.

We agree to find our hotel. It's another 20 minute walk along the promenade. Our guesthouse is The Inglewood at 26 Palace Terrace which is a tall Victorian building overlooking the sea. We are led up several flights of steep stairs to the very top in a four-bed room.

The thing the lads seem most impressed with is The Inglewood's close proximity to a pub with a beer garden. So we loiter for at least six minutes before we're sat in the beer garden. The view to our left is the Irish Sea: the view directly in front is a lovely pint of Okells ale, Okells being the main brewery on this fine isle. And then we get silly. "Shall we play pub golf?" asks Latta. "Well, it is McCully's birthday," chips Matt.

Pub golf is a drinking game that involves players each getting a pint in. Just like golf, a par is assigned to a particular pint. We suggest the first proper pint of the day is a par five. So if you drink it in four gulps you've managed a birdie, three gulps an eagle etc. Of course, what this means is we end up sinking several pints in quick succession.

We sample a few more pubs along the promenade before bargain hunter Latta sniffs out a deal. Bailey's Pizzeria is offering two-for-one on vegetarian pizzas. I'm ecstatic. This means I get a temporary rest from our round of golf and some vital food into the system.

Latta, aptly dressed in the Morrissey choc-ice "yummy" teeshirt, has always maintained the importance of food. During Liverpool FC European away trips he'd basically stop anywhere that was open: "Gotta get food when you can, Dickie. You never know when we'll get the opportunity to eat again."

Me and Latta look a right pair of indie kids. Tipping 40 and the both of us in skinny jeans and Converse. I don't think this whole Morrissey-galavanting, pub-golf-drinking, Converse-wearing, is us chasing youth. I think we found a look and a singer in 1990 that just stuck. At least that's what I'm trying to convince myself. McCully and Matt are dressed in respectable shirts. They look like they're off for a night on the town - which of course, they are.

Me and McCully finish our pizzas and take in the surroundings. Douglas seems lovely. We stare up at hills above the town as a mist rolls over. With the sun, San Francisco-esque fog, and a venue which looks like it belongs in San Diego, there's a Californian feel tonight.

Time is getting on. We should be heading to the venue. But a sports bar further towards town calls. Jaks is full of locals, I can't spot any Morrissey fans. I go to the bar and am amazed to see little TV screens attached to the beer pumps so you don't miss a moment of whatever sporting action is on. As I get the round in I notice there's a game on. It's Liverpool. They are in Norway playing Valerenga. I didn't even realise they were playing tonight. This shows how far Liverpool FC have drifted from my attention in recent years. The most important game at the moment is the pub golf and each of us is claiming victory.

We walk over to the Villa Marina. Fans outside enjoy the last of the early evening sun. The bar has a terrace which allows patrons to take in the sea views with a glass of wine. Inside, the venue is a sensation. A grand foyer, a large standing section surrounded by seats on all sides. We watch the pre-gig videos and take up a position far left at the front of the stage.

When Morrissey enters majestically in a black shirt, a huge roar goes up, a million flashlights: "Hello, Monte Carlo!" he pronounces to a frenzy of excitement. It's nice to be close to the action again after I was further back in York and Bradford.

I witness him sing the opener, *I Want The One I Can't Have*, for the fifth time since mid June. And it sounds as absolutely amazing as it did back in Inverness. Latta and Matt are to my right. Me and Latta sing ourselves silly to *Everyday Is Like Sunday*. Matt seems more subdued as he just gets into the experience and concentrates on the stage.

Midway through the set Morrissey comes close and Matt sees his chance. Matt leans, Morrissey leans, then Morrissey's hand, Matt's hand, together, gripped. The moment of destiny. It's just a handshake. But after our journey, the catamaran, the pubs, the banter, it's the real reason we're all here. It's just a split second as fan connects with hero and then it's gone. Matt is thrilled.

It's not just the music that inspires when you watch Morrissey. It's his moves, his words, his accepting mementoes and letters from the crowd. He is a joy to watch even without the music. Matt is not the only one on cloud nine. Morrissey passes the microphone to Gemma in the front row. She cheekily asks can she come on stage "for a hug". Unbelievably, Morrissey obliges. As the set comes to a close I notice Ian drift to the back of the venue. Morrissey ends with *First Of The Gang To Die*.

Outside Stephen Tait holds aloft a drum stick thrown into the crowd. Latta is having a Moz-crisis though: "Don't like the new songs at all. That *Scandinavia* song? Awful. I think he's finished." Me: "You're joking, he was amazing tonight, amazing."

Post gig we walk to the Sefton Hotel which has a bar inside called Sir Norman's after the legendary actor and comedian, Norman Wisdom. The walls are covered in screen shots and vintage memorabilia from Norman's career. It's all very Morrissey. And as fans talk about another fabulous night it becomes apparent that Morrissey is actually here. No, not in the bar, in his bed. Probably a few feet from here. Better keep the noise down then.

Debbie Allingham clings to a bottle of water used by Morrissey on stage: "It's his," she whispers, as if holding the crown jewels: "Do you want to touch it?" We have a couple more drinks then jump a cab back to The Inglewood. We stand on the promenade for a few moments and listen to the soothing sound of the tide. We stare back at the bright lights of Douglas. It is 2am and all silent. The promenade lights still burn bright and I'm sure some of them never, ever go out.

Tuesday 2 August 2011

Manannan does not depart until 3pm. So with time to kill Latta and Matt choose to wander to the opposite end of town. Me and McCully opt for a ride on the Manx Electric Railway. It reminds me of the cable cars in San Francisco.

The journey aboard the wooden tram as it climbs up to Laxey is relaxing. We pass through areas of beautiful scenery. We reach a tiny village and hop off for a cup-of-tea and a read of the local paper which paints a gloomy picture of unemployment with further job losses on the way.

By the time we have a walk around and catch the tram back it's late lunch. We bump into Gemma and Debbie who are still beaming from an awesome night. We talk about the moment Gemma got on stage. She says: "It felt like a dream. Morrissey smelt really nice. I believe that the Isle of Man is a magical place now after all that's happened."

Then it's time to head back to the ferry terminal. Reunited with Matt and Latta we board and take our familiar seat in the bar. No cans of ale this time. And then there's a familiar Moz downer. This trip and concert has been such a high and now it's time to come back down.

Debbie and her crew are aboard. Debbie says: "We got a smile and a wave, so we were made up with that."

"A smile and a wave, what do you mean?" I ask.

Debbie: "From Morrissey. He's on the ship."

Me: "What? Morrissey is travelling back on this ferry?"

Debbie: "Yes, he's sat upstairs in one of the private lounges."

A few other fans cotton on that their hero is aboard. One fan sneaks upstairs in the hope of a meeting then reports back: "I saw Morrissey. He's sleeping. Shall I go and wake him?" Me: "Are you serious? Never wake a man when he's asleep. And if that man is Morrissey that gives you even more reason to let him rest."

"Why don't you try first, Dickie? He knows you."

Me: "Morrissey doesn't *know* me. And I'm not going anywhere near him. I've met him a few times, what else is there for me to say to him? I'm certainly not going to bother him right now."

There's a game of cat and mouse going on. Two fans venture upwards and warn that Morrissey's security guy is keeping people at bay with a stare that says: "Don't even try." Us four just slouch back and relax. When we pull into Liverpool, we dive off sharpish while a dozen or so fans hang on for a glimpse of Morrissey.

The next gig for me and Matt is in five days time, this Sunday at London's Brixton Academy.

Sunday 7 August 2011

I'm not going to Brixton. I'd got back from the Isle of Man and my son, Frankie, was singing *Satellite Of Love* to me and quite simply I didn't want another weekend away from him. I had a dream about Morrissey the other night, it was his final ever gig and he was playing an Otis Reading cover. Maybe this indicates I've overdone the Morrissey thing this summer. So at lunchtime, when I should be on a train from Liverpool to Euston, me, Jen and Frankie are over in St Helens at Latta's son's birthday party.

We sit in the garden with cake as Frankie and pals jump up and down on a bouncy castle. Latta goes to his stereo, plays the three new Morrissey songs and concedes: "You know, maybe I'd been a bit harsh on Morrissey after the Douglas gig. The new songs are growing on me. They're not that bad after all."

We return home after a fabulous day to reports of rioting and looting in London. Matt sends a text saying that the atmosphere around Brixton is tense. It goes unreported in the media, but as London burns a Morrissey fan leaving tonight's concert finds himself in the wrong place at the wrong time.

Houston/ San Antonio

Monday 14 November 2011,
Majestic Theatre, San Antonio, Texas, USA

September 2011

It took all my powers of persuasion and exceptional timing. Matt had been eyeing Morrissey dates in Texas, America. I priced it up; £648 return with British Airways. Saturday 12 November: Fly from Manchester to London Heathrow. Then fly London to Houston, Texas. We'd catch three Morrissey shows in four nights: San Antonio Monday 14 November, Austin the following night, then Dallas on the Thursday. Fly back Friday 18 November. Simples, apart from having to broach the issue with Jen. She'd never let me go to Texas for a week. Would she?

I had to wait until Jen was in the best possible mood before I popped the question: "So, er, Matt is planning on spending six days in Texas watching Morrissey..."

Jen: "Oh, that sounds fantastic. Why don't you join him?"

I was gobsmacked: "What? Well it's a long way and I wouldn't really want to be away from home for a whole week..."

Jen: "Well, if you can afford it and want to go what's stopping you?"

October 2011

I sort the transport and concert tickets. I leave the accommodation arrangements to Matt. He gets some bargains, mostly cheap motels on the fringes of the three Texan cities. But the reviews are hardly glowing. Our two-night stop at the Days Inn, Downtown Riverwalk, San Antonio, is already filling me with dread. According to one dissatisfied customer on Tripadvisor: "This was easily the worst hotel experience I have had. We had to move to three rooms as the bed linens were dirty. One had fluid stains on the sheets. We finally asked them to just provide clean sheets. The sheets provided were too small and we ended up fighting all night to keep them on the mattress."

Another: "Not even close to the Riverwalk. Nasty looking rooms. Smelt moldy. Looked old and dirty. My dog would not even walk on the carpet."

It doesn't get any better: "I would not recommend anyone stay here. It's located right beside a train track and the trains run through the night - kept me awake. The front desk manager is very rude. I complained to the owner but he did not care. This hotel is in a bad area right off the freeway."

Gautam Shah, General Manager, has his work cut-out as he responds to half a dozen horrendous reviews: "We here at Days Inn strive to make every guest comfortable, please accept my apologies. We're in the process of remodelling (complete face-lift of the rooms)."

Oh dear, I'm not sure Matt has done his homework, but these places are only £20 a night. And it's somewhere to rest our heads. Anyway, what do we care? We're off to see Morrissey in the Lone Star State. Super-fun-times.

November 2011

It was supposed to be a routine check-up but after 45 minutes in the dentist's chair it was clear things were wrong.

"Mr Felton, you can wash your mouth out now." I gave my mouth a swill for an eternity before looking up for an explanation. "We carried out some root canal work and it didn't go exactly to plan."

Me: "What do you mean?"

Dentist: "One of the steel implements snapped and a little bit is now stuck in your gum. We've tried to get it out but we haven't got the tools to retrieve it. So I'm afraid that's where it will stay."

Me: "What? A bit of steel is stuck in my face? And won't ever be removed?"

Dentist: "Afraid so. It's perfectly harmless in there but we'll refer you to Liverpool Dental Hospital for further examinations."

Me: "Airport x-ray scanners."

Dentist: "Pardon?"

Me: "Airport x-ray scanners. Will this bit of steel set them off?"

Dentist: "Wouldn't have thought so."

Me: "Can you imagine explaining that one to over zealous airport security?"

Dentist: "I'm sure it will all be fine, Mr Felton. But I guess you won't know until you try."

Me: "Try? You don't understand. I'm meant to be going to Texas next week to see Morrissey."

Blank looks.

Me: "Morrissey? Music legend, ex Smiths, the greatest singer that ever lived. Me, Morrissey, airport, plane, America, Texas. You understand? I need to get there."

Friday 11 November 2011

I bounce along Liverpool's Dale Street, headed for my last day in work before America. iPod is blasting Morrissey's *Lifeguard On Duty*. A text from Matt: "Morrissey has cancelled tonight's gig in Chicago". Oh no, don't let this happen when we're set to fly 4,000 miles to see him. According to the True-to-you website Morrissey cannot play the opening date of his American tour at the Congress Theater due to a "visa administration error" involving guitarist, Boz Boorer. However, the other dates are good to go. Starting with San Antonio on Monday night.

Saturday 12 November 2011

I'm on the 06:59 to Norwich. The train is empty apart from three revellers who are on their way home after a night out. They appear to be living in a different time zone entirely: "I'm not ready to go home yet," slurs one.

Breakfast so far consists of a solitary Fisherman's Friend. Traditional menthol eucalyptus lozenges. Extra strong. First developed in the extreme conditions of the Icelandic deep sea fishing grounds. The packet tells of "invigorating qualities" manufactured by Lofthouse of Fleetwood Limited, Lancashire. Not recommended to children under five. They may as well put an 18 age limit on them. One taste blows your head off.

iPod on the go: Men at Work *Down Under*, Throwing Muses *Counting Backwards*, Inspiral Carpets *Two Worlds Collide*. I slump on platform 12 at Manchester Piccadilly which has a photo exhibition of the exteriors of the city's music venues. Some alive and well, some consigned to curry.

There's The Apollo, the venue for Morrissey's 50th birthday show in 2009. The Ritz, where it all started for The Smiths. The Manchester Evening News Arena is just a bland slab of concrete. Then one photo at odds with the others - an Indian restaurant - which was once The International.

Daylight arrives as my train rolls into Manchester International Airport. It looks like it's going to be a beautiful day - most of which I will spend travelling. I work it out; it's going to be a 20 hour journey all in. I get through security without any problems. No interest in my steel-injected gum at all. I get aboard my first flight to London Heathrow.

Terminal 5 at Heathrow is the business. Prada, Gucci, designer names, fine dining and class. I sit down for a beer at V Bar and take it all in. British Airways flight crew cruise past in pristine blue uniforms and chrome flight cases. "To Fly, To Serve" is the new slogan adopted by Britain's national carrier. An airline which is, in fact, part owned by Spain.

Matt appears; long dark coat, customary sports bag with very little in it and a huge grin. Glasses raised - Morrissey, here we come. Neither of us can truly believe it. One week on the road with Moz across Texas. It almost sounds too good to be true. Both of us are impressed with Terminal 5. It's polished and perfect. In vast contrast to other airports, there is a relaxed feel. It's a refreshing change. Even when the public address system announces the final call to Atlanta or wherever, it's delivered in a slow smooth style.

We amble over to our departure gate B38. BBC beams glum faces from Samsung TV's the size of snooker tables. The headlines are of the Eurozone Debt Crisis: *Silvio Berlusconi has vowed to step down after vote...*

Here we go, I show my boarding card and passport: "Welcome aboard, Mr Felton, Mr Crist, enjoy your flight." BA197 is a giant of a plane. I've no idea what type but it's a big 'un. We walk through first class as flight attendants pour champagne for well-to-do travellers. We head to our cheap seats: 52 G and H. Fab - near the rear - handy for the bar and the toilets.

We'd chosen seats on the BA website and now I understand why Matt insisted we sit near the back. I have four free seats next to me. I could lie down and kip if I wanted to. And I might have to at some point as the Captain announces: "There are 4,497 miles to our destination, flight time nine hours 24 minutes."

Right now, there's wine tasting to be done. We are served a 2011 Shiraz from South Eastern Australia. Matt's yapping to someone, I get my iPod on. Fine wine and Nick Cave *Into My Arms*, Fleetwood Mac *Second Hand News*, REM: *Nightswimming*. Ah, REM, there's a band for you. One of my favourites. Probably the first group which also sparked my interest in America. This will be my seventh trip across the Atlantic.

Not that my newspaper paints an optimistic picture of the land of the free. The Independent has a big feature by reporter Rupert Cornwell entitled: *"Is the American Dream at an end?"*:

> *"Ten years ago we had Johnny Cash, Bob Hope and Steve Jobs,"* runs a sour joke that has *been doing the rounds since Silicon Valley lost its most famous son. "Now there's no cash, no hope and no jobs." Perhaps not a contender for the Nobel Prize in side-splitters, but it catches America's dark mood – a year to the day before the country delivers its verdict on whether Barack Obama merits a second term in the White House."*

The US, like Britain, is stuck in an economic crisis deeper than anyone could have predicted. The article has tales of high unemployment, helplessness and homelessness. And here we are lavishly shelling out on a trip to Texas. We're the lucky ones, and I feel grateful to be in a job and be able to afford adventures like this.

The vegetarian meal comes around first. Unbelievable, this is a first for me. We're usually kept waiting until the carnivores have been served their animals; the cruelty-free meals tend to come out as an afterthought. Not today.

Next red wine up: Palacio de Bezares from Spain, then a third: El Muro Tempranillo Garnacha. You could say we are making the most of the free drink on offer. Matt's enjoying the hospitality: "Eight hours? I could do 80 hours on this flight." And then a slumber, a daze...

I come around. Where am I? On a plane, yes a plane.

Matt: "Oh, nice that you could rejoin us. You've been asleep for hours."

Minor hangovers aside, we feel top notch as we plant our feet on US soil. And what can be better on our teatime arrival than a huge queue to get through passport control? It happens every time you enter the land of the free and it gets no less painful. And so, for the next lifetime, we stand at immigration security at Houston's George Bush International Airport.

US immigration has a reputation for being unfriendly. At JFK I was once marched off to a room by men with guns who had the pleasure of rifling through my shirts, socks and factor 50 sunblock before allowing me in. Welcome to America.

Matt is in a flap. He's been in and out of the US dozens of times and is worried one day he will get turned away. It is at this moment we realise we are paying the penalty for being sat at the very back of the plane. We were last off and therefore last in the immigration queue. We trail back and forth planting our bags on the floor, then lazily proceed to kick our bags along.

Eventually Matt is summoned to stand in front of an eagle-eyed immigration officer and learn his fate. I'm stood ten yards away laughing. Matt looks under pressure. My laugh doesn't last long.

Matt, looking worried, shouts back to me mid-interrogation: "Do you know the address of the hotel were staying in?" I've no idea. It's actually looking a bit touch and go for a second before Matt gets waved through. I'm next - and equally scrutinised over not knowing the exact address of the nearby Ramada Humble.

"Er, the exact details are in my bag somewhere mate…" To be fair our interviewer is quite chilled. He nods me through and says: "There are thousands of Ramada hotels. Make sure you know the exact address next time." Big helpings of humble pie all round.

We are soon at the hotel with no address. It's on a freeway in the middle of nowhere. But it's nice, clean and welcoming. The lobby contains a huge star of Texas and a few wooden cowboys. Yee-ha.

It's early evening and within five minutes we're sat in the hotel's darkened bar with a couple of ice cold Bud Lights. They are as refreshing as can be. The Americans do cold beer very, very well.

Our room is big and overlooks a pool, volleyball court and small running track. We retire early after the epic journey and Matt has his iPad on so we can watch highlights of the 1985 FA Cup semi final between Liverpool and Manchester United. I nod off as Liverpool get a last gasp equaliser.

Sunday 13 November 2011

We are sat in the hotel's breakfast bar for 7am. Our bodies and minds in UK lunchtime mode. It's gonna take a day or so to get over the jet lag and into Texas time.

The TV news tells of a wife shooting her husband and how she's "likely to face charges later today". Then there's a big slot on the weather, then a report on another shooting, then yet more exclusive bulletins about the weather. ABC Channel 13 prepares us for 81 degree fahrenheit temperatures which are: "Unbelievable for this time of year."

Matt: "All we've heard about today is how hot it's going to be and that everyone is shooting each other." It's not long before we encounter our first weirdo. A man in a white shirt - half tucked into his trousers, half hanging out - does a jig past the bagels. Our eyes meet. I mutter a nervous: "Hi", he gives me a military style salute. I'm surprised he doesn't trip over - his shoe laces are undone.

At first I assume he works here as he starts tidying the breakfast bar. But he proceeds to take slice after slice of bread and then butter each with all the care of an artist crafting on canvas. Four, five, six slices later he's still sweeping the knife over and over again. It's starting to be a little unsettling. He puts the buttered bread into the toaster. He can't work it. This lasts for 20 minutes until he disappears down a corridor. "Shall we think about getting out of here and into Houston?" I suggest.

We take a cab to Houston. It's 20 miles and the journey takes half an hour. The freeway is lined with sex shops. An air freshener dangles from the rear view mirror and says: "I love Jesus".

We are due to catch the 11:55am Greyhound to San Antonio. We will see Morrissey tomorrow night at the Majestic Theatre. We arrive at the bus terminal two hours early. Our cab driver seems concerned: "Don't hang around here. Get yourselves into the terminal building and stay there. There's a lot of homeless people hanging around here and they target people like you."

We'd like to heed her advice but aren't prepared to spend two hours holed up at 2121 Main Street, Houston. Surely we can avoid a few suspicious characters to get a cup of tea somewhere?

Houston is closed. Sunday morning and nothing is open. It's bleak. A bedraggled woman in orange dress with hair all over the place lurches towards us and moans. Our pace quickens. Despite carrying our bags we are combatting the assortment of waifs and loons with a purposeful dart towards anywhere open. "Don't make eye contact", advises Matt. We don't, not even with each other.

Each corner brings another Houston stray. People sprawled on street furniture, slumped on garage forecourts; the city has a menacing feel. We walk for ten blocks and nothing is open. We crash out on a bus stop. Matt leaves his bag and goes it alone to find a cafe, a hotel lobby, anywhere remotely decent. I hope he makes it.

I sit on the sidewalk and gawp at the shiny steel skyscrapers that surround. I bet Morrissey and crew aren't encountering the same problems. I bet they are safely settled in some plush San Antonio hotel ahead of tomorrow night's gig.

After five minutes Matt wanders back and punches the air in celebration just like United striker Frank Stapleton did in last night's YouTube re-run of a football match from 26-years-ago: "I've found somewhere!"

Thank god for Ziggys. It's a hip cafe-cum-bar which is light, bright with local art on the walls. The waitress is humming to a Death Cab for Cutie album playing in the background. What's playing on the stereo can speak volumes about a restaurant.

Matt tucks into quesadillas and three pints of Coke. It's thirsty work all this trekking around Texas. I go for a veggie burger and chips. It's still only 10.30 but in reality we are tucking into lunch or even dinner. It's the jet lag - our bodies telling us it's later than it actually is. We feel it's best to stuff our faces now while we have somewhere open. The bus trip to San Antonio is three hours so best to get fuel on board while we can. I can't see there being many food options aboard.

We go through security at the Greyhound station and it's a bit unnerving. "Where are you from?" asks security guy: "Liverpool, England."

"What's in your bag? Any knives?"

Knives? Gosh. This Greyhound experience is already frightening and we haven't even boarded yet. We've heard some horror stories about the Greyhound but it seems to be the only way to cover the first two dates of the tour. It's cheap and the timings are good.

Today's bus trip is the longest we'll have to do. San Antonio to Austin on Tuesday will only be 1.5 hours on Greyhound. Wednesday's trip to Dallas is aboard the Amtrak and we will journey in luxury on that six hour leg in something called a 'deluxe roomette'.

We get seats near the rear of the coach. It's full but not heaving. No nutters, thankfully.

As we pull out of Houston we pass banks and churches, millions of them. Matt falls asleep. My only entertainment for now is the road signs: "All I want is a Buc-ees shirt - 33 miles," then: "Hey buses - 49 toilets - in 33 miles." Then there's a classic: "It's good to have a lot of bull in you."

So, this is Texas, the second most populated state in America. Home to 26 million people. Its 260,000 square miles make this single state bigger than the whole of Britain. Flat land - big skies - to be fair we could be in Lincolnshire. It takes exactly two hours twenty minutes before we spot our first ranch. Cowboys! Cattle! Lots of them. At last, we are born.

The boredom is creeping in. Talk moves on to the real business - tomorrow's Morrissey gig. Matt recounts a tale of him watching Morrissey at New York's Bowery Ballroom in March 2009: "I got five handshakes off him that night. I was nearly in tears."

It seems Matt has had no problems getting touched by the hand of Moz. I think Morrissey clearly recognises him at shows, and Matt's a tall lad, so he has a greater wingspan than most fans.

We stare from the Greyhound. There's a Little Red Barn steakhouse. Little? It's the size of a football stadium. We reach downtown San Antonio. It looks nice. It's great to get off the bus and stretch our legs. We consult a map. Our hotel looks a fair way away. We grab a taxi and drive away from the nice part of town through some distinctly dodgy looking areas.

No sooner are we on a busy expressway then we turn off the busy expressway and give each other a nervous glare. This place looks dodgy. We sweep into the forecourt at the Days Inn Downtown/Riverwalk which should be tackled under the Trade Descriptions Act as it's nowhere near Downtown or Riverwalk.

A man is in the hotel car park going through the bins. The welcome at the "downtown" Days Inn is anything but. The lady on reception takes an age to find us a room. Strange, the hotel is hardly busting at the seams.

Once we check in we go to our room which is at the rear of the building, facing wasteland and a railway. It's bleak. But it has a pool and it's hot. We decide to don trunks and sit by the water. But who in their right mind can relax by the pool when yards away roars the freeway? This is a surreal place. It's bizarre that just hours ago we were in the English winter and now we are dangling toes into a pool surrounded by palm trees. But this is far from a paradise. The layer of grime and the million drowned insects afloat on the water mean neither of us fancy a dip.

We last 20 minutes before heading into town. We go on foot and walk extremely fast. This part of town is grim. Run down shops, a few chain hotels. By contrast San Antonio itself is beautiful. It seems relaxed, clean and friendly.

Riverwalk is a sunken man-made canal that bends and weaves through the city centre. Like a modern Venice but with palm trees, bars and restaurants. We try to get into the Hideout bar which seems to have its entrance through a gift shop. Bizarre.

We enter the sparse looking gift shop but where is the entrance to the bar? We try a cupboard door, no luck. This is weird. We can't work it out. Suddenly what was a mirror opens. Two members of the pub dive out, hand us hula hoops and insist we try them before being allowed inside.

When we walk into the bar we get a standing ovation which is fantastic and frightening in equal measure. We get a beer and look up at the TV screens. Now we understand. Our hapless efforts to enter the pub had been beamed live. It seems that making tourists look silly is the national sport in the Hideout. It's hilarious. We then watch several tourists suffer the same fate before being allowed in. Who says Americans haven't got a sense of humour?

We spend the rest of the day and night exploring this fine city. We head to the Alamo. It looks like a small castle. The Battle of the Alamo in 1836 was one of the key events in the Texas revolution. The Alamo was the scene of a 13 day siege as Texan forces held firm against the Mexican Army. The place is now a museum and its floodlights light up the white stone giving it a dramatic appearance. The Texas flag flies proudly above the Alamo. In fact, Texas flags fly everywhere in this stunning city. And what a flag it is too. Red, white and blue with a single white star.

Pat O'Brien's Irish Bar has a lovely courtyard with flames leaping from a fountain. Inside runners relax after competing in today's San Antonio half marathon. Everyone sits outside. It's mild and a massive contrast to rainy England. In the distance the bagpipes can be heard. Everyone is out on the streets walking and enjoying the balmy evening.

We slide back down to the Riverwalk. The first bar is playing Johnny Cash *Ring Of Fire* and both of us clink glasses and sing along. The bar stools have the Texas flag. It's just red, white and blue everywhere. Welcome to the Republic of Texas.

We have one in Dick's Last Resort (well, with that name can you blame us?), before it's back to the Hideout bar which we've decided is probably the greatest bar in the entire world. A chilled-out band performs on stage at the end of the room. The singer plays his acoustic guitar beautifully. And then it's time to slip away.

Monday 14 November 2011
Majestic Theatre, San Antonio, Texas, USA

I wake to the sound of freight trains outside. Tonight is the night. Morrissey at the Majestic Theatre. We don't really want to hang around in the Days Inn for long.

Before we know it we are back in downtown San Antonio and take a walk around the venue. Morrissey's tour bus is outside and it's the first visible sign that this is really happening. A few fans loiter outside the stage door. We collect our tickets from the box office. We've got hours to kill before the main event.

We get some provisions at Walgreens on Houston Street. And we bump into Morrissey fans Cathy McCartan and Tom Haupt. Cathy was my ticket saviour in May 2009 at the Manchester Apollo for our hero's 50th birthday gig. It's great to see her again. Cathy, 56, tells us she had travelled to Chicago on Friday only to be left disappointed by the Moz no-show. "I was originally going to do Chicago only, but when you mentioned that you and Matt were doing the Texas gigs I thought it would be fun to see my fellow cult members. Plus, I had never been to San Antonio or Austin. And, it's just as well I decided to come here after Morrissey cancelled Chicago."

Cathy explains that she befriended Tom a few months ago on Facebook: "I liked his sense of humour, and when Tom mentioned he was considering going to Texas, I contacted him and asked if we could travel together and share expenses." Both Tom and Cathy are wearing Moz tees. Adorning Tom's left forearm is a tattoo with one word: Morrissey. He has driven all the way from Florida to San Antonio for tonight's gig. That is a journey of more than 1,000 miles.

Cathy has put in a fair bit of mileage too. She flew from Asheville, North Carolina to Charlotte then onto Chicago. And then Chicago down to San Antonio. Cathy only discovered Morrissey in recent years yet her devotion to the man is breathtaking. She has thus far seen him eight times including two trips to Britain. She's had her fair share of bad luck on the Moz trail with five gig cancellations and two abandoned concerts (Swindon when Morrissey collapsed and at Liverpool Echo Arena thanks to one idiot and his beer bottle).

Cathy's story about how she discovered Moz is extraordinary: "I only heard of Moz in November 2008 when I happened upon the 2004 Quarry interview with Jonathan Ross on YouTube. It was addiction at first listen and I immediately bought all of The Smiths and Morrissey albums the next day," says Cathy.

"The first tour dates announced, which I immediately booked, were London and Manchester and the next date announced was….Asheville, North Carolina, where I live. Unfortunately 2009 wasn't the best year to become a Morrissey addict, since he was ill for a bit of the tour."

Matt is a bit stunned: "So, you only first heard Morrissey three years ago? And now you're following him around the US and Britain?"

Cathy: "Yes. Seeing him live is an unbelievable experience that transports you to another universe."

Cathy's ambition is to meet Morrissey and get him to sign her arm for a tattoo. But the main talking point at the moment is mine and Matt's transport plans over the next five days. "Greyhound? Amtrak? Are you serious?" asks Cathy. It seems that car is king in America. Public transport? You've got to be joking!

It's fantastic to see Cathy and Tom, but it's time for lunch, so we vow to see them at tonight's show. More sightseeing, I drag Matt to the Tower of the Americas. It looks like Berlin's TV Tower or Liverpool's Radio City Tower or any other tower for that matter. The 750ft structure has a restaurant and bar on top. And what a view. Simply stunning. You can see for miles. You can see our hotel; I can almost make out someone rifling through the Days Inn bins. The bar is spectacular. A restaurant underneath revolves. This is a great place to relax and prepare for Morrissey.

Back on street level and then down once more to Riverwalk which is pure tranquility. Walkways, little bridges, beautiful gardens, wooden decking, palms, a statue of St Anthony (San Antonio) with a yellow rose left at his feet. By early evening we are in another Irish Bar on Riverwalk: Waxy O'Connor's. It's happy hour. We sit outside and watch the world go by. This truly is a wonderful town. Inside an acoustic guitarist begins playing a David Gray cover. I'm wearing a Liverpool FC tracksuit top and as I walk past singer, Joe Walmsley, he breaks off mid song and shouts: "That lad's got a Liverpool top on!"

Once Joe's finished *Babylon* I go over and say 'hello'. Unbelievably it turns out that Joe is from Liverpool. The musician got a job performing on cruise liners in 2001 and in recent years has been the resident artist in this fine pub. Joe's life is now firmly in Texas; he doesn't get back to Liverpool much. There is a 60s vibe to his singing. I can see why the locals like him. Waxy's has Joe play here five nights a week and the singer is grateful for them supplying him with generous amounts of Murphy's Irish Stout.

Me and Matt enjoy happy hour and watch day turn to night. As it gets busier and busier we get excited about Morrissey. What will he play? What will he say? Suddenly my heart skips as Morrissey's PA appears and sits down nearby. Oh my God. Morrissey wouldn't show up here would he? Not a few hours before going on stage? I play an hypothetical game of 'would I go over if he turned up?' Would I just leave him alone? It's all academic as Moz is not around.

Me and Matt head back over to the Hideout, which I work out is the third trip to this bar in two days. It's getting towards 8.30pm and it really is time to go to the Majestic. Matt wants another beer: "Come on mate, Morrissey won't be on stage for at least 40 minutes yet." I have a feeling we should go in and I just about manage to convince Matt to do the same.

We get searched entering the theatre. Mid-frisk I hear a song. It sounds a bit like *You're The One For Me Fatty*. I turn to Matt but he beats me to it: "That sounds like…*Fatty*…"

Me: "It can't be?" It is: Morrissey is already on stage. Matt's face is a picture. He goes white with shock. So let's get this straight: we travel more than 4,000 miles for a concert, we arrive two days early, and still manage to miss the start of the show. Shocking.

We sprint in. We are miles from the stage, stood behind the mixing desk. Morrissey looks like a tiny dot. We try to take in how we could have let this happen. There's not much point even trying to find our seats as it's pitch black save for the bright lights of a few dozen camera phones filming Morrissey's every move.

He plays *Speedway* then *Ouija Board, Ouija Board* as we watch from a distance. From what I can make out he looks in fine form. Tight black v-neck jumper. He sounds and looks sensational. The band play to perfection and the music takes me away from the disappointment of our late arrival.

Matt shouts into my ear above the noise: "Right, let's make our move." We show our tickets to security and walk down the centre aisle. People are dancing everywhere. There's a few empty seats, we dive in. As he plays *Maladjusted* my eyes get more used to the light, and the Majestic is a stunning venue. Ornate, gothic, grand, it looks like an underground temple from an Indiana Jones film and it's very, very hot. The girl next to me keeps shouting: "Morrissey, I love you, I love you, I love you." I think my eardrum is going to burst.

Maladjusted sounds terrific. The sound strong, Morrissey stalks the stage. The crowd goes crazy. I can barely make out what he says after this song. It seems everyone around me wants to shout at Morrissey that they love him.

I Know It's Over and the girl next to me is beside herself in tears. Morrissey has the audience in his hand and in his heart. For the encore, *Still Ill*, the Majestic goes absolutely mental. We find ourselves very near to the front and Moz is just yards away. People are screaming at the top of their voices at the sight of him so close. The song moves into its final minute and that's when the excitement builds beyond words; there must be hundreds here who are weighing up a bad rush on stage.

A girl makes it stage right. The one lad, Paul, who is English, manages to get on stage for a lovely hug with Moz. A few more also get lucky in the frenzy; some get a touch, others are intercepted by security and sent spiralling. And then it's over.

Outside there is the familiar buzz. It had been an incredible concert. Me and Matt go back to the Hideout (well, where else did you think we would go?). As I walk in the the DJ is playing *Suedehead* - my favourite song of all time. Bud Light anyone? How I love San Antonio.

Interlude 6

"I travelled from my home in Singapore to see Mozzer in concert for two nights at London's Royal Albert Hall in 2002. I spent both nights waiting in vain to meet him outside the venue but did end up meeting Boz, Alain, Mozzer's mum and his sister.

"Morrissey's mother Betty was a sweetheart and she was gracious and polite when I thanked her for raising such a talented man who is loved by many around the world. The flight from Singapore to UK took 13 hours. I decided to go all the way to London because Moz was without a record label (at the time) and he hinted that he may quit making music. So I quickly bought the concert tickets online, booked the flight and travelled to see my number one idol.

"I bought everything on sale at the merchandise booth. I burst into happy tears when he opened the first night by singing my ultimate favourite Smiths song *I Want The One I Can't Have*. I tried sneaking backstage (using an expired Access Backstage Areas pass) but the bouncers booted me out, much to my utter dismay. During one of the two nights I waited for him, I did see a large car coming out of the venue. It stopped for about 30 seconds with someone in the backseat looking out at us. It was much too far for me to make out who was in the backseat, but I would like to think it was Le Moz surveying his adoring disciples waiting out in the cold for him.

"About 10 years have passed since this 'pilgrimage' and many things have changed about me - for the better. My love for Morrissey still prevails and endures."

Melanie Oliveiro, Singapore

Austin

Tuesday 15 November 2011,
Bass Hall, Austin, Texas, USA

Tuesday 15 November 2011

San Antonio Greyhound station looks like a huge public toilet. Navy tiles on the walls. This is hot, stuffy, smelly. People divided into pens lining up for buses. No chairs anywhere. Why sit down when you can just stand up queuing? This is like travelling Ryanair but in baking conditions.

There are bags and belongings everywhere, and a random mixture of passengers. The Austin queue seems full of young people, a few students travelling light. The other queue has some people carting their whole lives with them. Destinations are announced and buses leave to Laredo and Monterrey. The bearded man next to me has assorted plasters on his hands and ears. We gotta get outta here. Just announce the Austin bus, please...

We finally get aboard. This bus should have left 35 minutes ago. Thank God this is our last bus trip of the tour. Our driver looks frazzled. I don't have much confidence in him getting us to the live music capital of America. One hand on the wheel, one hand on his mobile. He spends ten minutes chatting as he negotiates his way out of the city.

Tonight Morrissey plays Bass Hall, Austin, but all that concerns us is getting there in one piece. It's raining. We get on the freeway. The weather worsens. And then our stressed bus driver takes us over unmanned rail crossings. No barriers, no flashing lights. Our driver just gets his bus and us on the track then looks left and right down the line to check that some thunderous freight train is not about to smash us into oblivion.

This is scary. Now thunder, lightning. The bus stops in a small place called San Marcos which looks bleak. Shacks, graffiti, aimless souls like zombies stalk the bus station. Ahhh, let us out of here. "Elect Gerry Nichols for San Marcos City Council" say the banners on the roadside. I think he will have his work cut out.

We are now in a fully fledged storm. It's 10.30am but it may as well be 10.30pm. The sky is pitch black and it's getting worse. The constant swish of the bus windscreen wipers is trance-like. This is the most depressing part of the trip so far. The road to Austin feels suicidal. And in true 'Dickie Felton panic style' I'm starting to fear we are not headed in the right direction at all.

Matt: "This is unbelievable. Almost like the end of the world." I'm biting my nails and sweating: "I know. Do you think we are on the right bus? It's just taking a long time. San Antonio to Austin is meant to take one hour 15, but we've been on this for two hours already and I haven't seen a single sign for Austin." Matt: "Me neither." Finally we see a huge billboard for Harley Davidson Austin. Relief all round. Why no road signs for cities? You could be going the wrong way down a freeway for weeks.

Super 8 Austin Downtown is not too bad a motel. Situated on a freeway slip road. At least we can see the city from here. Downtown Austin looks like it might be a 35 minute walk away. It's good to just dump our bags, and the welcome here is warmer than at the Days Inn San Antonio.

We find our room. It's the usual affair. These cheap motels seem to follow the same formula. Decent sized room, twin beds, tiny bathroom, the door opening out to a car park. We don't hang around. Within minutes we are heading to the famous 6th Street which we're told is home to nice restaurants and bars. We need to eat. After 20 minutes, and for the first time all day, the rain stops and the sun comes out.

Our mood gets better once we hit 6th Street. We enter a fabulous restaurant and have a great lunch. The waiter keeps filling our glasses with Diet Coke. I take two sips and he's back to fill it up. We'll end up drinking ten pints the way he carries on. "I don't know what we went through on that bus trip this morning, Matt. I've never felt as depressed in my entire life." Matt agrees: "I know, it was horrible. But we're here now and Austin feels great."

We wander into the Driskill Hotel. What a magnificent and haunting building. It has a look from a completely different era. And it is, built in 1886 by cattle baron, Jesse Driskill. It has ornate balconies and a grand facade. Inside, the Driskill is dark and atmospheric. Over a pint of Bud Light I feel tempted to get a new tattoo. When I last watched Morrissey in America in 2007, I met him outside the venue in Royal Oak and he signed my arm. I had it inked immediately in a nearby tattoo parlour. And now, I'm on another Morrissey tour, and I'd like another tattoo. I did see a place a few blocks down...

We give Black Cat Tattoo a go. We've only been in Texas three days, but we already feel an affinity with the Lone Star State. As the needle makes contact with skin, Matt winces and he can take no more. I wouldn't mind, but it's me getting the tattoo, not him. After about an hour we are done. Now a part of me will forever be Texas, the state flag to flutter forever on my upper right arm.

It's mid afternoon and we take a walk out towards Austin's Bass Hall which is on the University of Texas campus. We want to pick up our tickets from the box office, just so we have them in our hands. The campus is the size of a small city. Absolutely massive. What we thought might be a 20 minute walk has already taken more like an hour. We're not bothered though. It's nice just to walk and relax in the sun.

We come to the home of the Texas Longhorns college American football team. It has more than 100,000 seats - for a college team - unbelievable. The biggest stadium in England is Wembley which has 10,000 fewer seats than this giant. We finally find the Bass Hall which, in keeping with everything being bigger than we expect, is a huge modern glass auditorium.

And outside sat on the steps is Margaret Gonzalez, the fan I met in York back in June. Margaret is on home turf, a native Texan. She is with her pal and they are sat forlornly on steps near the stage door. Margaret: "We saw Morrissey come in but he didn't stop."

Matt collects the tickets for tonight's show as we wish Margaret well and make our way back to the Super 8. We get freshened up and opt for an early evening dinner at Mexitas, which is just over the road from the motel.

With its bright green neon Mexitas certainly stands out. And it needs to, as it's located well away from the hub of 6th Street. Once inside initial thoughts are that it is more warehouse than restaurant. A huge space and we're the only diners in here. The welcome from proprietor Jose Uriegas is instant and warm. He's straight over with drinks. When he discovers we are English he immediately offers us complimentary Tequila. When I tell him I'm vegetarian Jose instructs his chef to prepare lots of different animal-free dishes.

The food is amazing. Jose pulls up a pew and joins us. More Tequila, he's now brought the bottle over. What a guy. Matt gets stuck in while I politely decline. We chat about England, Mexico, Austin, the economy. Even if we didn't have Morrissey in a few hours, this has already been a tremendous evening.

Jose's hospitality extends to offering us a lift to the Bass Hall. Unbelievable. We finish our meal and the friendliest restaurant owner I've ever met gives us a lift in his motor. The three of us complain about the economy on both sides of the Atlantic. Jose is interested to know English petrol prices.

I leave the gas talk to Matt; he's a driver not me: "I guess if you work it out, in England we're probably paying the equivalent of around nine dollars a gallon now." Jose is stunned: "Oh, my God. We're paying around $3.17 a gallon. England's how big? About 200 miles wide? To cross the state here you'd travel 850 miles. That's why everybody has big cars. But these poor truck drivers now are getting just six miles to the gallon."

Matt's turning into quite the economist: "That's it. There's the knock on impact on trucks that take food and goods to shops. And the cost is passed on to you and me. So everybody ends up paying more." Jose: "But it is relatively cheap to eat in the US. Austin is not pricey, San Antonio is cheap. I go to Phoenix and it's having incredible problems with its economics, and to eat there is more expensive than here."

We arrive at the Bass Concert Hall. We shake hands with Jose and wish him and his fabulous restaurant luck. Right, we've a concert to go to. The venue is pretty cool, art work on the walls and an incredibly hip crowd. This place seems very much like the Bridgewater Hall in Manchester.

The Austin concert goers tonight are incredibly stylish. Some dressed as if they are at a ball; frocks, dresses, black tie. San Antonio seemed a bit more rough and ready. There are some great tattoos on show. Many tattoos of the Texan flag. I'm glad my new ink means I've joined the in-crowd this evening.

I get two beers, they cost $6 each. Ouch, the most expensive beer of the trip so far. Matt smirks: "That must be painful paying that, Dickie, after we found places in San Antonio selling the same ale for about five dollars less."

We bump into Cathy and Tom; they are very excited for the gig. We tell them we'll meet later and go down 6th Street. Two lads come over with smiles the size of longhorns. They waited for Morrissey at his hotel earlier today and had their copy of *Bona Drag* signed.

We get inside. This venue seems huge. Three tiers of seats seem to stretch back all the way to San Antonio. We take up a position near the front rail, far stage right. The bells chime, he's on and screams: "Amigos, Amigos, Amigos!" And we're off again. *I Want The One I Can't Have* the usual opener. We are much closer to Moz than last night. I have a great view of him. His shoes? What shoes is he wearing? Since age 17 I've been fascinated by Morrissey's wardrobe. And on this rare occasion I'm so close I can see his footwear. Fantastic black pointy shoes.

There's a scrum of photographers in the pit who fight for the best shot of the man. After the second song they are ushered away. How I love *Action Is My Middle Name* and how I love singing along to every word. It takes *Everyday Is Like Sunday* to really get the crowd going. "For God sake, whatever happens, keep Austin weird," says Morrissey.

Post gig we dive out and meet Tom and Cathy. Tom's car is a sight to behold; etched on the rear window in Old English style is: "Morrissey US Tour 2011". We hop aboard the Tom-mobile and hit 6th Street. The four of us are in agreement that it had been a fabulous show albeit less rowdy and crazy than last night. Tom reveals he had travelled to Scotland for a few of the dates last summer including Dunoon. Me: "Now that was a night, Tom!"

Austin is home to more than 200 live music venues and right now we are in the loudest, with some rock group determined to deafen us. I'm all for a bit of loud rock but not at the expense of my eardrums. We move to a quieter spot next door. Tom, is resplendent in cream jacket and Moz tee, Cathy has the "It's Morrissey's town" tee on. The four of us are pretty tired after the last two days of the tour. But the pints fly to the background sound of the very wonderful Coldplay single *Paradise.*

Before we reach a karaoke bar we bump into several Morrissey fans. One is clutching a sleeve from Morrissey's red shirt from tonight's gig. Moz had thrown it into the crowd during the show. Another fan rolls up his sleeve to reveal the singer's signature the length of his arm. Amazingly a few of these American fans were also in Dunoon. How on earth do they do it?

Before I can quiz them further we're in a bar and Matt is eyeing up the karaoke. "Do you think they'd let me sing a Morrissey song?" I bet him $20 he hasn't got the bottle to take to the microphone. He proves me wrong. And for a moment me, Cathy and Tom feel like we're back in the Bass Hall as our stars-in-his-eyes singer belts out *The First Of The Gang To Die.*

Dallas

Thursday 17 November 2011,
McFarlin Auditorium,
Dallas, Texas, USA

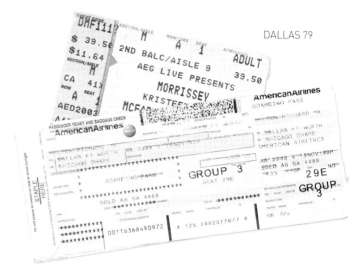

Wednesday 16 November 2011

Up and out at speed and feeling rough. We didn't get in until the early hours. Thank goodness for Texas licensing laws which make it illegal for anywhere to sell alcohol after 2am.

Today it's onward to Dallas which is a six or seven hour train journey. It's getting to be a bit of a drag unpacking the case, then repacking the case, then when we leave somewhere making sure we've got all our belongings, tickets and passports. I've been losing paperwork as I go - deliberately. As soon as we've left one motel I've destroyed all the maps, address details, bus tickets. On a trip like this the paperwork almost outweighs your clothing. Not that I packed many clothes. I'd brought with me old teeshirts and jeans so once worn I could dispose of them. The plan was for my bag to get lighter as the trip goes on.

And so, the Amtrak. Austin train station consists of one basic waiting room. For a city this size it's a bit of a let down. I mean, I wasn't expecting London St Pancras, but I've seen Hornby model stations bigger than this. Our train is meant to depart at 09:31 but it's running late. A giant Union Pacific freight train thunders through, bells ringing, pulling about three hundred trucks. Trainspotting can't be big over here; you wait days for train and when it arrives it goes on and on and on.

Finally, ours shows up. The grandly titled *Texas Eagle*. We make our way to the sleeping car. Helpful Amtrak staff carry our bags. Good start. We are led to a Superliner Roomette which is basically a mini compartment for us to relax in. The two chairs turn into bunks. This is what you call travelling in style.

But no time for sleep. Breakfast is being served. Our onboard train manager Tony Clementi seems like a character and welcomes us with a feast fit for kings in the dining car. He's fast talking and funny. In his uniform and specs he reminds me of Tom Hanks in the Polar Express. He offers us a beer. "No way," I say instantly. "Oh come on Ricardo, you know you want to," urges Tony. The train to Dallas is already looking like a fine move. Orange juice, coffee, cheese omelette, potatoes, cakes, all included in our $65 fare.

I reckon I only had about five hours sleep last night, so decide that the bunk may be a good idea, at least for an hour or so. Before I pull the curtains across I notice that the slightly weird passenger in the roomette opposite is reading *Pure Murder* by Corey Mitchell. It slightly unnerves me. As the train shudders and lurches no wonder I find it difficult to fall asleep.

Mid doze I wake to the sound of train manager Tony with an "important announcement": "Will passengers Felton and Crist make their way to the dining car as lunch is served." More food aboard the *Texas Eagle*. Lunch is splendid and I'm surprised at the big vegetarian selection. Black bean and corn veggie burger, greek salad. You don't get this back home on Virgin. Me: "So Tony, what time will we reach Dallas?" Tony: "We may get there at 4pm or 5pm or later, who knows?"

I start to question the vagueness over timings but it quickly becomes apparent how difficult it must be for Amtrak to keep to exact times. The distances covered provide a clue. The *Texas Eagle* is travelling the entire length of the US. From San Antonio in the south to Chicago in the north. The journey will take a staggering 22 hours. So it's almost impossible to say exactly when a train will arrive at a stop along the way.

Big Tony downstairs in the snack bar is doing his best to drum up custom for every calorific snack under the sun. Every once in a while he gets on the public address to advertise his "Candies, pretzels and potato chips." I imagine that if you were on this train for the full 22 hours you'd eat your entire bodyweight in junk food.

Never once is it announced how the train is behind schedule or what time we'll reach Dallas. If you have a young family the Amtrak just wouldn't be an option. Stations with no facilities, trains which may or may not turn up. But for us, on this sunny Wednesday, it's ideal. We don't see Morrissey again until Thursday. For the next few hours we just recline in the viewing car.

Our train eventually rolls in at tea time. The last moments aboard the *Texas Eagle* and we're ending it where we started seven hours ago - in the dining car. I'm excited: "Will we pass the place where JFK was shot?" "Yes the train goes right past Dealey Plaza, you will see it to our left," says ever helpful Tony Clementi. I give an enthusiastic: "Oh great!"

Tony laughs sarcastically: "Oh yeah 'great' Ricardo, getting excited about a man getting his brains blown out..." I didn't mean to sound so kiddy about a place where a man lost his life. But this is the site of massive historical importance and like everybody else I've watched the documentaries, seen the Oliver Stone film and been intrigued as to what really happened.

Time to get off the *Texas Eagle*. I had my bags packed about an hour ago ready to dive into Dallas. Not that I'm desperate for our rail odyssey to end, I'm just keen to experience a new city. Matt is still supping a Bud Light - in no rush to do anything. If it wasn't for the Morrissey gig tomorrow both of us could quite happily stay on the Amtrak all the way to the Windy City. Travelling by train in the US is fabulous.

How could so many citizens of this wonderful and crazy country be so apathetic to rail travel? I lost count of the frowns and sighs we received in Austin when telling people we'd be hopping aboard the train for this date of the tour. Compared to Britain, the trains here are sensational.

We wave our goodbyes to Tony and his Polar Express. Stepping down onto the platform the chill hits us immediately. Dallas is several notches colder than Austin. We walk about three blocks and are at Dealey Plaza. This is it. The place John F Kennedy was assassinated.

I'm struck by how, 40 years on, the place looks exactly the same as it did in all the old newsreels. Very little has changed around here since 22 November 1963. I expected to see a McDonalds or a Wendy's, but Dealey Plaza is exactly as you'd expect it to be. There's a few people milling around. Photographs get taken, people loiter near the white fence on the grassy knoll: a location cited by conspiracy theorists as being where a second gunman fired at the President.

Despite its horrific past and six lanes of traffic, Dealey Plaza is green and peaceful. A few street vendors tout souvenir newspapers of the assassination. The Plaza is named after George Bannerman Dealey, an early publisher of the Dallas Morning News and civic leader who died in 1946. Yet the place named in his honour is synonymous with an infamous murder.

Anyway, enough of JFK for now. We need to hunt out our motel. As usual, it's cheap as chips and a little way outside downtown. Not that this is much of a problem; the gig tomorrow is on a university campus north of Dallas and our place is up that way.

I amble with little purpose. Matt is more direct and darts across a pedestrian crossing while I get stuck at a red light. From across the road I see he's successful in hailing a cab. By the time the lights change and I catch up he's already deep in conversation with the taxi driver. And while it may be a full six weeks until 25 December, we have landed in a sleigh, I mean cab, driven by Father Christmas. "I am Santa" proclaims our taxi driver. Oh no - not another lunatic. We've only been in this city five minutes and we have a cabbie with a split personality.

But no, our driver really is Santa, well, for four weeks of the year anyway. He gets dressed in red, decorates his cab and spreads season's greetings across Dallas. He sounds like a lovely guy until we drive through a somewhat depressed part of town: "You know, there are people here who will rob you, stab you and kill you."

This is not exactly the kind of festive cheer I was expecting from Lapland's finest. I'm not sure whether he is referring to this particular neighbourhood of Dallas or America in general. There's something totally disturbing about a taxi driver issuing this kind of safety advice because taxi drivers tend to be in the know. Like our driver in Houston. There's none of the obligatory "But every place has good parts and bad" reassurances, St Nick just paints a bleak picture. Our nerves rise as we slide onto the freeway headed to our last motel of the tour. Please let this be in an area we won't get robbed, stabbed or killed.

Hurrah, the Best Western Cityplace Inn looks survivable. We make plans to shower and hit a restaurant and some bars, assuming there are any. I'm thirsty - I haven't touched a drop all day. But for the very first time this tour Matt is out for the count. Sprawled on his back, he isn't going anywhere. Even the party maestro needs his kip sometimes.

Thursday 17 November 2011
McFarlin Auditorium, Dallas, Texas, USA

Matt: "I can't believe I fell asleep. Why didn't you wake me. I was all set for a session."
Me: "Sorry mate, there was no rousing you, you obviously needed your sleep."

Truth is I didn't try to wake him at all. I was totally shattered and needed a night in. I was almost relieved he was zonked. But today - our last day and night in America - will be different. We'll go out with a bang and watch magical Morrissey live tonight at the McFarlin Auditorium.

We walk to Downtown Dallas. There's an amazing amount of building work going on with cranes everywhere. I've always viewed this as a positive; it means a city is in good health. Dallas Museum of Art has a brand new exhibition: *The Fashion World of John Paul Gaultier: From the Sidewalk to the Catwalk*. It features over 140 haute couture dresses.

We fancy taking a look, but it doesn't open for an hour so we wander instead. We have the entire day at our disposal and it's the last day, which means we're keen to pack in as much as we can.

"Strange Dallas, isn't it?" I observe, "You know, we've been walking for an hour from the motel to the centre of town and we haven't seen a single person." Matt: "Where is everyone? It's not like it's a Sunday. This is Thursday, isn't it?" Of course, there's millions of people sat in cars, mostly stuck in the same traffic jam, but no pedestrians. There aren't even any shops; I had been looking forward to clothes shopping. But instead it's just skyscraper after skyscraper. At last, people. We spot some construction workers building another skyscraper to stand alongside the million or so others. But there's just so few people anywhere. Strange.

We eventually get to the memorial to John F Kennedy. It looks like a huge art installation. White walls surround a granite slab which bears the name of the dead President in gold letters. It's a beautiful spot, meant for reflection. We arrive to find a party of young schoolchildren having their lunch sat on top of it.

We head to the Sixth Floor Museum at Dealey Plaza which chronicles the assassination and legacy of JFK. The 48th anniversary of his murder takes place in a few day's time and the museum is busy. Me and Matt don headphones and take in the audio tour. Museum staff look like nightclub bouncers. The word 'security' on teeshirts puts you ill-at-ease immediately. Maybe that's the whole point. We were issued with a stern warning about not taking photographs or video.

The most remarkable thing about this museum is that it's located in the building where Lee Harvey Oswald fired the shots that changed history. And in the corner, separated from museum visitors by perspex, is the very window from where Oswald pulled the trigger. In the souvenir shop they sell replica beads like the ones Jackie Kennedy was wearing on that fateful day. On the carriageway outside 'X' marks the exact spot where bullets hit their target. We watch some motorists swerve so not to drive over the very spot where '*it*' happened.

The City Bar, Dallas lightens the mood. Christmas lights adorn a large mirror behind the bar as a 50s crooner croons on the stereo. We sip ice cold cans of lager. There's a pop art poster of Johnny Cash on the wall and the Texas flag, of course, hangs proud.

We hop next door to a posh-looking hotel to see a bus outside. Not any bus; the Morrissey tour bus. Wow. Morrissey and band must be staying here. We settle at the bar as staff put up the Christmas tree. It's all very festive and it's fitting to get an expensive bottle of red wine in. Suddenly, we spot Boz Boorer and Jesse Tobias getting aboard the bus.

Me and Matt have some philosophical banter about what exactly are we doing 4,000 miles from home following a pop star. By the end of the conversation we both agree that it's just something we do because it's just we something we do. And, well, it's just so much fun. The red wines start to flow, and when Matt isn't looking I decide to do something very silly. I source paper and envelope from the hotel receptionist and I pen a brief note to our hero:

> *Dear Morrissey,*
> *It's Dickie here from Liverpool. We are following the tour from San Antonio to Dallas. You have been amazing. We've loved watching you this week and as tonight is our final night I was wondering, if possible, could you shake Matt's hand during the gig?*
> *Yours sincerely,*
> *Dickie Felton*

I hand it to the receptionist and it's a very surreal moment as I say: "I was wondering, could you get this to Mr Morrissey?" Receptionist: "Certainly, sir. I will make sure he gets it right this minute."

Me, in a sweat and a panic: "Er, well, you don't have to get it to him straight away..."

Receptionist: "No, I insist, he's in his room so I will take it now to ensure he gets it."

Within a split second I rejoin Matt at the bar, tell him nothing of my letter-writing and suggest we head off, quickly. Anyway, it's early evening and we don't want to be late. We have a quick freshen up at the motel then hit the road on foot, headed north to another university campus. We walk alongside a four lane freeway in the general direction of the McFarlin Auditorium. We have no real idea where we are going. The receptionist at the Cityplace Inn just pointed in the general direction. Up and out of the city and towards the university. We end up walking through some nice suburban areas.

Matt sees the sign first and stops stunned: "Look at that. A bar called Strangeways. Can you believe this? We are 4,000 miles from home on our way to a Morrissey gig and accidentally stumble upon a bar named in his honour?" This bar looks like an old mission, or an old shack, a bit like the Alamo but smaller. "Matt, I just don't believe it. Come on, the Strangeways must refer to something totally different. A bar in a suburban street in Dallas, Texas, would not be named after The Smiths' 1987 studio album. Would it?"

We walk in. And then jaws drop as we gawp at a selection of Smiths' sleeves on the walls, and photos of our hero everywhere. We don't even say a word to each other. We just pull up a stool at the bar and try to take it all in. The owner, Eric, shows up and we introduce ourselves. Eric is the man who has transformed what was a beat-up bar with a bad reputation into something altogether more charming. For the first time this entire trip we are served real ales. None of that Bud Light stuff. "...and so you named a bar after a Smiths album?" I ask, "That's just genius."

Eric shows us photographs of him with Morrissey. He went to the star's home when he was living in Los Angeles. "I'm not like one of these fans who hang around waiting for Morrissey to sign their arm," Eric says. I lie: "No mate, me neither."

The talk goes around that Morrissey was in Dallas today getting his hair cut and allegedly insisted that the barber mop up all his hair and give it back. Laughs all round. A story so wild, it's probably entirely true. Eric seems like a top guy and offers us a lift to the gig via a few other bars in the neighbourhood. By the time we show up at the McFarlin we are slightly worse for wear. Like Austin on Tuesday, we find ourselves in a cleaner-than-clean university campus. Eric drops us off near the venue while he parks up. The McFarlin-looks a bit like the college in James Dean's *Rebel Without A Cause* - all steps and brick.

Inside we bump into Cathy and Tom. And two British fans: Paul, who made it on stage in San Antonio, and the ever everywhere Stephen Tait. Another all seated venue, we just loiter with the rest of the hardcore Morrissey fans near the front of the stage. We watch Kristeen Young's set and she's fabulous. At first Security seem happy to let fans stand where they want. We are exceedingly close to the stage, stood behind Stephen and Paul. The venue has a stage which protrudes a little in the centre allowing Morrissey to get as close to his fans as possible.

The bells chime, Morrissey walks on and declares: "We have come to occupy Dallas." Then, although it's a familiar set, we just marvel at seeing him again and being close. Thousands of miles from home we just want to savour every single second. *You Have Killed Me*, *You're The One For Me Fatty* sound as good as ever until I feel a tap on my shoulder. "Let's see your tickets. Are you sure you should be stood here?" Security suddenly gets tetchy. Matt's all in a flap: "I haven't got the tickets, have you?"

Somewhere rooted in my denim jeans in a crumpled mess should be my ticket. But I turn to Paul and Stephen in front, "Er lads, I don't suppose I can borrow your tickets for a split second?" I flash the two tickets and Security seems to accept them. All's fine but as we enjoy *First Of The Gang To Die*, Security moves back in: "Can we see your tickets again?" This is getting stressful. I turn to Paul and Stephen again, but it looks like we've been rumbled. May as well just accept that Security wants us to move back to our seats.

Until, Morrissey stops mid song, turns to the four of us and says: "Are you all OK?" Moz then beckons his own security guy to tell the McFarlin local Security to piss off. What a fantastic moment. As the set nears the end Morrissey comes close and seems to make a beeline for Matt. His arm stretches; so does Matt's. It's a re-run of Douglas as hands clasp together. I wonder if..? I wonder if Morrissey got that letter? Maybe it hadn't been such a bad idea after all.

Before he launches into the final song Morrissey says: "I'm sorry you've all been strapped to the floor, but you're not old enough to be trusted by yourselves." The band bursts into *Still Ill* as assorted bodies propel themselves towards the stage. Morrissey sings and touches as many hands as he can as we enter the last moments. I decide it's my time. Matt gives me a lift, I hit the stage. I miss Morrissey, Morrissey misses me. Security pounces. My body dragged off.

Slumped over pizza with a sore left wrist, me, Matt and Cathy reflect on a fantastic gig. Tom's not happy with the heavy handed security; neither am I. But Morrissey had sung well, the band had been great and it had been another sensational night.

But as we wait for a cab back to our motel, all I can really think about right now is home. I haven't seen Jen and Frankie for a week. We get back to the motel. "Right Dickie, let's have a nightcap in Strangeways. Come on, it's the last night." Me: "I'm finished Matt, it's time for bed."

Friday 18 November 2011

We are on separate flights today. While I head home to England, Matt has a few more days in America to visit friends. I explain to the taxi driver that Matt's flight is at 10:00, while mine's not until 14:05 so he needs to go to Matt's terminal first.

But not for the first time a Texas taxi driver has us in a spin. "No, wait a minute, if one of you wants to be dropped off at Terminal One and the other at Terminal Three that's a problem. These terminals are miles apart. I wouldn't want you to miss your flights."

From what he is saying Dallas Fort Worth Airport is the size of a small British city - probably bigger than somewhere like Milton Keynes. "Mate, it's fine, drop Matt off and I will just get off with him at his terminal. My flight is not for hours, so I can wait." Taxi driver, determined to complicate and confuse matters: "But the terminals are miles apart, what I can do is take one of you to Terminal Three and one of you to Terminal One…" For the first time all trip me and Matt speak at the same time, loudly: "Just drive will yeh."

The road to Fort Worth is littered with conspiracy theories; taxi driver is convinced there were multiple shooters on the grassy knoll. He even has diagrams to prove it, which he unveils while doing 100mph along the freeway. We emerge from under his diagrams and souvenir JFK assassination newspapers to arrive at our terminal.

And so this is it. Six days, four cities, three Morrissey gigs, 54 songs, one handshake, one failed stage invasion: our American adventure is almost over. Matt goes through security with Philadelphia his next destination. I hope the bars are ready for him.

I need to catch a flight to Chicago where I have a 40 minute wait before catching a plane back to Manchester, England. The girl at American Airlines is certain I will have time to make my connection in Chicago. "Oh don't worry, sir. American Airlines is never late." "That's good to know, but I only have 40 minutes changeover time to get my Manchester flight." "Mr Felton, relax, it will all be fine."

And so I do relax; magazines, breakfast, lunch, a few nervous stares at departure boards. And then I notice: 14:05 Chicago DELAYED. Apparently there's horrendous weather in Chicago which is delaying flights. I go to the American Airlines desk: "As things stand, if I miss my connection I'll not get back to England. Is there any chance you can get me on an earlier flight out of here?"

Several other travellers are trying the same thing. And so there's now seven of us on the reserve list for three places. What had been a relaxing wait has now got tense. "Hang in there, Mr Felton," assures the American Airlines girl: "We'll do our best to get you out of here." I can't help but smile: she's making it sound like we're in the movies and I'm escaping some kind of nuclear armageddon.

I pace the gate, glance up at the departure board, I do some more pacing, I bite my nails,

I check my phone for the millionth time. "Ok, Mr Felton - you're on - here's your boarding pass."

I get to Chicago O'Hare International early and the airport has Christmas in full swing. Huge Christmas trees, lights everywhere. It's very seasonal and in a very warming way, just nice. The last leg of the trip. I board another American Airlines flight. First fail on my part, I didn't reserve a seat. And so I find myself in the worst ever spot on the worst ever plane. I'm rammed in the corner next to two huge blokes. The leg room is minimal. There was more room in the back of my old Renault Megane Coupe. Seven hours of torture. How on earth am I going to deal with this? Why didn't I just book with British Airways coming home? Why didn't I try to pre-book my seat?

My iPod on, I listen to a Desert Island Discs' Tony Adams interview. Then I read a magazine I picked up in Dallas: Best Homes In America, 150 pages of the most inspiring homes. This is torture. Seven hours to go, six hours to go, five hours to go, four hours to go, three hours to go...

Dallas...

Interlude 7

"The Twitter Mozarmy happened very naturally one Friday night in December 2010. Tweets from fans were being exchanged about gigs, pictures, facts and song lyrics, so I said: "lets hashtag our tweets 'Mozarmy'" and the fan understanding and following just grew from there.

"#Mozarmy spread incredibly rapidly around the world. In a few weeks we had followers from LA to Sydney. One month later we opened @Mozarmyquiz: ten questions about The Smiths or Morrissey, winner hosts the following Friday. We have ex-members of Morrissey's band, authors, photographers and celebrity fans get involved and participate in this unique community. Some have hosted the quiz and donated very precious prizes.

"There are relationships, friendships, meet-ups and club nights. There are Mozarmy babies, dogs and doll effigies. There are discussions of gigs, lyrics and sharing of pictures. One fan (@cyborganisation) found out that despite seeing The Smiths and Morrissey I had never managed to grab a piece of his shirt so he sent me a small chunk of his.

"These are the kindest people you've never met, all with one thing in common; a love of Morrissey and The Smiths. So one day, if you're bored...by all means tweet."

@marriedtothemoz

Julie Hamill, London

Rome

Saturday 7 July 2012,
Cavea Auditorium, Rome, Italy

Friday 1 June 2012

When I turned my back on the Trevi Fountain and flicked Italian lire over my right shoulder, the tiny splash indicated I'd be back some day. That was February 2001 and now, 11 years on, I was preparing for my fourth trip to the Eternal City. All roads return to Rome.

We'd been debating whether to make the trip to Italy for Morrissey's show at Auditorium Cavea on 7 July for two months, but Ryanair was asking £160 return which was too much so we'd abandoned plans.

That was until Matt noticed flights had dropped to £60 there and back. As quick as you could say 'gatti di Roma' we'd booked. Two nights, a Friday, a Saturday and Mozalini live in a modern amphitheatre. Can you imagine that stunning spectacle? Morrissey playing in a beautiful venue in one of the most beautiful cities on earth.

Rome plays an important role in the Morrissey story. The singer lived here for a while at the Hotel de Russie off Piazza del Popolo. The 2006 album *Ringleaders Of The Tormentors* is basically an Italian album. The record references *Piazza Cavour* as polizia sirens sound. *Ringleaders* was inspired by and made in Rome.

When Morrissey was photographed outside the Pizzeria La Montecarlo six years ago, the restaurant became as much of a Moz landmark as Salford Lads Club. While a pizza place is hardly as inspiring a backdrop as the Lads Club was for the famous *The Queen Is Dead* photo, it attracts Morrissey fans on a daily basis.

Not all my Rome memories are entirely positive. As a Liverpool supporter in 2001 we ran the gauntlet of knife-wielding Roma thugs when we travelled to the city for a UEFA Cup tie. Two goals from Michael Owen sent the Ultras into a rage. They torched cars, stabbed more than 20 of our fans, and hurled bricks at our coaches. I think this is what you call the famous Italian passion. Still, despite that experience, I'd always seen beyond the football. Rome to me is all about fine wine, scooters, ruins. I'd been struck by the magic of the Trevi, the colour, the noise, the Peroni.

The transportation will be Ryanair. I know, I know, "*Ruin-air*" - what on earth am I thinking? Budget plane travel = a nightmare. But when it's only £60 return you have to put up and just do it.

Friday 8 June 2012

The absolute bastards. The complete and utter violation of our home. It's an horrendous scene: every drawer emptied, belongings everywhere, family jewellery stolen, 20 of my shirts missing. And the worst of all, our two-year-old's bedroom ransacked. There had been a spate of burglaries in the area and while we were away at my sister's wedding, vile scum had entered our house with an axe. They'd taken our possessions, but the worst part is the knowledge that they'd been in our home going through our things. They'd stolen football souvenirs, watches, rings, but bizarrely, had turned their noses up at my signed Morrissey collection. No class, clearly. Scumbags like these have probably never heard of Morrissey.

In anger I draft an open letter to the burglars and send it to the local newspaper:

"I'm not sure what the worst part was. Finding our new home invaded and ransacked?

Realising you'd been through our two-year-old's Batman bag and toys? Maybe seeing your axe left next to my boy's Thomas the Tank Engine? Were you prepared to use it on us had you been discovered? You took lots of precious things: the gold signet ring my great uncle gave me. Uncle Harry is not around anymore but he wore that ring in World War 2 and he and this band survived the Battle of the Atlantic, but it didn't survive a break-in by you.

If you look into this precious item - now in your grubby little hands - you may see an inscription on the inner band: "From Mam 1932". I hope the tenner or so you got for this has been well spent. You also took my white Bose iPod player. Sorry to inform you mate – it doesn't work. I can't believe you didn't spot the 200 Euros on the table but took the empty Gucci glasses case instead. Pal, you need an eye test, usually free for scroungers like you. The iPhone 3 box you nicked - yeah, sorry sucker: empty. The Wii Fit box? No handsets! I just wished I'd filled the Glenmorangie whisky you nabbed with something else of a similar colour which doesn't taste as sweet." Dickie Felton.

Anyway, I decide not to do Rome in a month's time. How can I leave Jen and Frankie at home alone while I travel to Italy? The thugs could come back. I ring Matt and tell him the bad news.

Sunday 10 June 2012

Ok, maybe I'm overreacting. I can't just stop going away from home on the off chance that burglars could strike. I ring Matt and tell him Rome's back on.

Tuesday 3 July 2012

As the rain pours down in Queen's Square, Liverpool, I bump into fellow Morrissey fan David Lewin, 42. He's due to see Morrissey too in Rome this Saturday. He's flying out with Jet2. He'll also stay in Italy for the Florence gig a few days later. He's done 16 days back-to-back at work to fund the trip and he can't wait: "The *Ringleaders* album was written in Rome so it's going to be so special to see Morrissey there. I want a teeshirt too, I'd kill for one with Italian dates on it."

Thursday 5 July 2012

It's off. Frankie is poorly with chicken pox so we'll have to take turns in looking after him until he gets better. What a nightmare. But I can't be swanning off when the poor thing is ill. I ring Matt and tell him I can't go,which as you can imagine, goes down like a lead ballon.

Friday 6 July 2012

Frankie's feeling better. Jen: "Why don't you see if there are any flights going out tomorrow? It's not ideal but at least you'd get to see the gig." I search the websites of Ryanair and British Airways. Nothing doing. That Ryanair flight Matt took this morning doesn't operate on Saturdays. BA has flights going from Manchester to London and then on to Rome - but the hassle and cost - an eight hour trip and £400 is just a non-starter. I'd get to Rome maybe in time for the encore.

Then I remember what Dave Lewin said when I met him on Tuesday morning. He was flying to Rome with Jet2 from Manchester. I check the budget airline's website. There's a flight leaving at 7am tomorrow, direct to Rome. But the fare shows up as £269. Did I really want to see Morrissey in Rome so badly I'd fork out a small fortune on top of the money I'd already spent? It's a crucial 'make your mind up' moment. Cogs frantically turning in my head. Cost: £269 plus the cab ride from my house to Manchester Airport. It would top £300. Could I? It's a huge amount of money for just 24 hours in Rome.

I return to the Ryanair site. Could I do Liverpool to Dublin then Dublin onto Rome? No, it just isn't viable. I go back to Jet2 still undecided. And then I do a double take - the extortionate flight I had originally considered has just been slashed in price. Instead of £269 it is now £139.

Note to self: Dickie, either book it this second or condemn Auditorium Cavea to the regrets file at the back of my mind for eternity. That was it, mind made up. I grabbed my bank card and frantically tapped the numbers in. Morrissey in Rome, here I come. I text Matt: "I'll see you tomorrow, get the Peroni in."

Saturday 7 July 2012
Cavea Auditorium, Rome, Italy

My alarm goes off at 4:45am. Taxi driver smiling on time and he's in a hugely spiritual mood. As we zoom along the M62 past Ikea and Marks and Spencer there's barely another vehicle on the road. We both see the sun rising over St Helens. Driver: "I love this time of day. The beauty of the light, the moment night turns into day. So many people never, ever experience this."

And so this on-off-on-off Morrissey adventure to Rome is definitely back on. Crazy really, when you consider that yesterday lunchtime I was going nowhere slowly. A taxi trip I was expecting to cost me £65 comes in at £40. I get that feeling that this is going to be a great day. Everything is going for me. I'm at Manchester Airport in plenty of time. A healthy porridge and skinny latte provide the fuel. Flight LS791 departs at 7am.

The bar in Terminal One seems busy. Some people on lager. I love that airport time zone - when it's morally acceptable to drink at any time. I decide to give a beer a miss, at least until I'm on Italian soil. After a five minute delay I'm aboard and quickly discover another advantage of buying my flight ticket at the eleventh hour. I've been allocated a seat with extra leg room in row five. I stretch out and wait as the cabin crew announce they have champagne to buy for "anyone celebrating a special occasion".

It's some private celebration I'm enjoying at present. I'm 37,000 feet up, barely believing I'm going to see Moz tonight. A cup of tea in my hand as we fly over Zurich, I strike up conversation with the couple next to me. Both in their 50s and from Manchester, they are set to catch a Royal Caribbean cruise ship in Rome to enjoy a week sunning themselves around the Mediterranean.

The couple are quick to sell the whole cruising experience; the gorgeous food, the on-board facilities, a different city to visit every day. I do like the sound of it. And I think one day we'll give it a shot - if we can combine a Morrissey date in one or more of the ports of call. The husband, a taxi driver, then adds: "These big cruise ships have the lot nowadays - including big shopping centres. It's like sailing around on the Arndale Centre." How anyone would think that spending their holiday sailing around on something akin to a Manchester shopping precinct is good is beyond me. But the couple seem adamant it's a supreme experience and I'm not one to argue.

"I'm going to see Morrissey in Rome," I boast. "I will be in the city for a full 22 hours before flying home again. A quick in and out to see the Manchester music legend." Taxi driver: "Why on earth do you want to go to Rome when he's playing in Manchester in a few weeks?" I just laugh. Captain updates us on progress and how we'll follow the coast past Pisa before descending to Rome. I listen to Frank Sinatra and Supergrass on my iPod. Over the Alps, I switch to *Ringleaders*. Even *In The Future When All's Well* (one of my least favourite Morrissey tracks) is sounding sensational. It takes just over two and a half hours before I emerge down the steps and into the Italian sunshine. The heat, fabulous.

I dart through immigration fast. No hanging around, I've got to live every minute of this. I get to the train station. There are two trains heading into the city. A slow one which stops everywhere and costs next to nothing and a fast, direct train which costs 14 Euros. As I'm sat aboard the quicker of the two (was there really any option?) I just take in the beauty and colour. I've left the drab rain and greyness of northern England behind for 90 degree fahrenheit Italy. Bright flowers in fields, palm trees line the rails, while homeless people living under bridges indicate another side to the place.

The train is so smooth it literally glides through the 25 minute journey into central Rome. I step onto the platform to a sea of people. Termini station is a noisy, bustling place. Supermodel-esqe teens lounge on walls, a few waifs and strays hassle tourists for money. I return inside, grab an ice cold beer from the fridge and sit in Ciao bar on a balcony. Within seconds Matt arrives. Handshakes and beaming smiles. We made it (in the end).

It's noon and we have just 20 hours in this city so there's not much time to waste. Matt tells me his solo night out last night here was quiet and he's keen to make amends today. We'll see what we can do as we stride to our nearby B&B.

Wait! A toy shop. A red Rome fire engine and blue police car bought for Frankie. Matt buys himself some new insoles for his shoes. With all the pacing he's been doing on this tour his shoes have reached the end of their journey.

We dump the bags at the Trinity B&B which is reasonably central at 109 Via Emanuele Filiberto. Blink and you miss it. The Trinity is located on the third floor of an apartment complex. We need three sets of keys to get into the place. Once inside it's fine. Huge room, ensuite, high ceiling with window overlooking the road.

Walking again. Like we've been doing this entire tour. Walking through Douglas, walking through Dallas, now walking through Rome. We grab a couple of beers from a little shop and sit by ancient Roman ruins taking in the noise and the beautiful blue skies. We find the most un-Irish bar I've ever entered. Huge letters above the door boast an Irish welcome. Inside, just one solitary Guinness sign. The place doesn't even seem to sell Guinness. With so little time and so much to do, we don't settle long. We need to find the Pizzeria La Montecarlo to recreate that famous Morrissey photograph.

My map reading skills on this tour have been first class (if I do say so myself). But as this trip was "off" for a while I didn't plan properly and have no map. This makes our search for the restaurant harder than first anticipated. A five minute hunt turns into 25 minutes. After an exasperating and fruitless search I'm ready to throw in the asciugamano (towel). My dummy is hurled from my cot: "Oh, let's just sack it off. We can't find the bloody place, my map reading is crap and I'm starving." Matt: "No, let's carry on looking. It can't be far."

Ten more minutes aimless wandering and in desperation we hail a taxi. Our Roma cabbie seems to have an idea where the restaurant is but proceeds to speed up and down the same street four times. Meter ticking, it's the shortest and yet most expensive cab ride in history. "Jesus! Twelve Euros for that!" yelps Matt in disgust. Now it's his turn to get irate.

Anyway, we made it. Just off the main drag is the La Pizzeria Montecarlo. I salivate at the thought of Italian food in our hero's fave pizzeria. We arrive to find it totally and completely shut. It is a totally unremarkable place. Down a side street that no-one can find, with dozens of award stickers on the outside for good food. Pity none of us can actually try it.

More cursing and gobs on until we bump into two Morrissey fans having the obligatory snap taken outside the premises, too. Dubliners Joe Kelly, 44 and brother Nick, 41 are doing the same as us: as ridiculous as it sounds - making a pilgrimage to a pizza place.

Cameras are exchanged and we get several photos of each other leaning against the wall alla-Morrissey. Talk moves onto the gig until we get interrupted by a tiny car trying to squeeze past Pizzeria La Montecarlo and a bollard. It's a tight squeeze and it's touch and go for the young brunette in the driving seat. Me and Matt are trying haplessly to steer her to safety: "Left a bit, right a bit, back a bit." She's about to collide stone with steel until a local comes to her rescue and let's us get back to the important banter.

Joe and Nick tell us they first saw The Smiths in 1984 at Dublin's St. Francis Xavier Hall (SFX). They were aged just 16 and 13. That night was the start of something special.

Joe: "The Smiths were the first group we ever saw. Morrissey was the first and we've followed him ever since. I go to around 70 or 80 gigs a year by all kinds of bands. I'm a fan of all music but Morrissey has a special place in my heart. I don't have the time to go from country to country like some of the fans manage to do. But I try to go to about four or five of his gigs each tour."

Like us, the Kelly brothers fancied Rome and the chance to watch Morrissey in this wonderful city. Nick: "For us, we like to do the travelling thing as well as watching Morrissey. The gig is part of the experience."

Joe: "And it's still fascinating watching him sing and the whole interaction with the fans. I love his vocal nuances and the subtle lyric changes. His voice gets better and richer with each passing year and his new songs continue to be consoling and very witty. It's wonderful to see the new generation of young fans coming through. That's something I wouldn't have expected."

Asked if they have any interest in meeting Morrissey at this stage, Joe replies: "I met him backstage at my first gig in 1984 and got my ticket signed, so that's good enough for me".

Anyway, the most pressing matter now is finding somewhere to eat. We shake hands with the Kellys and spot another pizzeria across the road. Food at last. And a huge headache I can't shift. I'd been battling with a heavy cold all week and at the worst possible time it is coming home to roost.

We take a cab ride along the banks of the Tiber up towards the venue. It's a good ten minute drive. There's a serene scene outside the modern looking Auditorium Cavea. The venue seems to be on a complex of other concert halls and facilities. Fans sit on a steep grass verge, some fans sit on a terrace supping lager in the warmth.

A lad from Bolton appears and tells us he's taken a week off work to follow Morrissey across Italy: "Travelling, fine weather, fine music, just me, Moz and the open road." Clearly a man after our own hearts.

There is a sizeable British following here tonight. David Lewin and partner Michelle are sat around a big table of Morrissey fans enjoying the early evening atmosphere. The Liverpudlian first met Michelle at the Star and Garter club in Manchester at a Morrissey/Smiths disco in 2010. David says: "We got together because of Morrissey. We travelled to his gigs as friends at first but then things developed. Morrissey does bring people together."

I can't get over the number of people on this tour that have got together through Morrissey. I wonder if he is even aware of the matchmaking effect he's had on his support? David has seen Morrissey 18 times. But he was a fairly late developer. He only got to his first gig three years ago in 2009: "I'd been a fan since 1993 but before the internet it was hard to get tickets. Plus, I had two young children at that time and they were the priority so I just didn't go to Morrissey gigs. You could say I'm making up for it now."

And here comes Margaret Gonzalez with pal, Gloria. I'm totally amazed at the number of shows these two get to. Margaret in particular has popped up everywhere from York to Dallas to Italy. In the month of July she is taking in nine Morrissey shows in five countries: Italy, Greece, Israel, England and Scotland. It's a staggering show of loyalty to Morrissey.

There is a party atmosphere outside the Cavea. A young, hip crowd loiter. There's a book shop and bar outside the venue. The Italians leaf through books, the British get on the ale. It's such a fabulous and chilled out spot. There is none of the queuing stresses like other gigs. People just hang around, chat and contemplate a night with Moz. We get our Liverpool FC/ Morrissey flag out and photos get taken. A group of Italian fans have their own flag with the letters 'TIALTNGO" on it. This stands for *There Is A Light That Never Goes Out*. It's like a football match with the home and away fans getting their flags on show and getting along just fine.

I've had enough to drink. A bad head, a long day, I'm tired. But this is Morrissey in Rome so it's time to move. We enter the venue. The Cavea layout is similar to the York Barbican. Big wide stage, an upper tier of seats, some standing at the front. And it's totally open air. The Cavea staff seem happy to let fans stand or sit where they like.

We get a position at the front, stood behind Chris Wilde and Stephen Tait. We watch support act Kristeen Young. Save for Dallas, I've never watched an entire Kristeen Young set. Tonight, it's different. Me and Matt stand transfixed as she sings magnificently. Yellow dress, long black hair, her voice piercing and perfect as this European day turns to night. Kristeen has been a long-standing Moz support for five years or more. I've watched her dozens of times but tonight it really seems to click. She drags and sweeps the microphone stand across the stage and sings with purpose and absolutely beauty. "Matt, why have we never properly appreciated Kristeen Young? The times we have missed her because we've been sat in pubs..."

Once Kristeen's set is over Stephen Tait turns to me and for the first time this tour it's my turn to face a few questions: "So, Dickie, who do you love more, Morrissey or Liverpool FC?" "Gosh, Stephen that's a tough one! It's not an easy question to answer at all. Years ago I'd have said Liverpool FC but I'm not so sure anymore."

To my right is German, Annelie, who has travelled from Berlin. To my left is an Italian fan who is holding back the tears at the thought of Morrissey's imminent arrival. The lights go down and the intro song gets played: *Imperfect List*. Amid strobe lights Morrissey enters and the crowd goes mental. Flashlights, screams, the bloke next to me is bawling, Anneile shaking: "I can't believe he is this close."

Morrissey looks menacing and mad-for-it: "Mama Roma, Mama Roma, Mama Roma" his opening address to the disciples. It's into *Shoplifters Of The World* then *You Have Killed Me* which sounds the best it has ever done. *I Know It's Over* is beautiful and the Italian lad next to me is a blubbering wreck. Morrissey in sky blue shirt with a jockey-style "V", looks amazing. Boz Boorer, in drag and a dress, looks amazing. The set is exactly the same as usual, the emotions are exactly the same as usual. It's wonderful. I must have heard *How Soon Is Now?* a million times but it sounds better and better and better.

During the last few songs, many try for the stage. In the chaos Margaret Gonzalez and pal Gloria seem to get a hug off Morrissey. Then it's all over. Outside, my headache reaches epic proportions. Me and Matt dive on a bus, any bus, that looks to be headed home. I notice a few British Morrissey fans who I last met at his gig in Madrid in 2008, but I'm too tired to even say 'hello'. Our bus eventually pulls up at Termini. I help myself to three pints of Diet Coke and collapse into my bed at The Trinity.

Sunday 8 September 2012

As my train pulls into Liverpool Lime Street an email pops in from someone I've never met:

"Oh well. A little presentation: I am in 1966 and I am a criminal lawyer, known as "Ultras' lawyer" cause very often I defend hooligans. I follow Morrissey since 1986 but at that time he didn't play in Italy so often, so the first time I could see him live (no low cost flights at that period!) was in Nonantola, near Modena, in 1999 if I remember well.

"Just wanted to say that finally Roma showed his real face at the Auditorium gig yesterday, with crazy fans jumping on stage and singing along with Moz. Despite the age, I felt like an adolescent, and only because – at last! – I could shake his hand, I didn't invade the stage.

"No matter the age, no matter the job, no matter if you're alone following him in the other four Italian dates, leaving your wife home with three little children: this is Morrissey, dear, and it is a religion."

Avv. Lorenzo Contucci

Rome...

Interlude 8

"OK this is my story. I know it's naïve, I'm not a good writer. And my English is not very very good, but I'd like to share it with you. I don't care if it's gonna make it to the book, these primary thoughts are for you really. Book or no book. YNWA.

"I was a boy when I started this trip with him in 1984. Now I am 43 and Moz is still here. The only standard through all these years in my life. During high school, university, army, jobs, relationships, in good times, in bad times, through wins and loses from my team.

"Found friends, lost friends, through him. He has been my best and sometimes my only friend. He moulded my taste in life. I have seen him eight times, last time July 2012 in my favourite open theatre in Athens in Lycabettus Hill, a place full of memories since I go there since childhood.

"The strongest moment was when I grabbed his shirt in one piece during Athens 2006 gig. I'll treasure it forever. What more could I ask for? A Smiths reunion maybe?"

Dimitris Antoniou, Athens, Greece

Manchester

Saturday 28 July 2012,
Manchester Arena, England

Friday 27 July 2012

Life is for living. It seems that the world is in motion and headed to Britain. The Olympic Games is kicking off and the opening ceremony features music from The Beatles, The Jam, Rolling Stones, The Specials, David Bowie, Queen, Sex Pistols, New Order, Frankie Goes to Hollywood, Soul II Soul, Eurythmics.

It's a glorious musical trip from the 1960s to the present day. Happy Mondays, Prodigy, Trainspotting - *lager lager lager*. Then *I'm Forever Blowing Bubbles* (the famous West Ham United chorus), Blur, Dizzy Rascal, Amy Winehouse. British musical culture is getting one hell of a run out in East London in front of a global audience of one billion. It sounds and looks amazing. But of course, Morrissey and The Smiths are completely absent.

There's only one ceremony that matters come tomorrow for 20,000 disciples. After a three year wait for Moz to play in his city, he is home. It will be like a football team bringing home the cup. A celebration, a party, our hero returns from pastures far.

Morrissey has played to sold-out crowds all around the world in the last 14 months. Chile, Japan, Hawaii, Europe, America and of course Dunoon. Last week it was Israel tomorrow he plays next to the Arndale. The Manchester Arena (once known as the Manchester Evening News Arena) is not quite sold-out. But it's damn near it, which in the current economic climate is amazing. There will be thousands of us there.

Saturday will be the ninth time I've seen Morrissey play Manchester. We need to go back two decades for my first experience of watching Moz play in his home town. Christmas 1992 at the rough and tumble Apollo. In those days the venue was all-seated which led to frustrations among the crowd who wanted to basically go crazy. I managed to get to the tiny standing bit at the front. *Suedehead* struck up, I had a leg up and I crashed into his arms. I was promptly shown the door. I got back in - paying £15 to a tout. It would be 12 long years before Morrissey returned to the city. I never realised so many Morrissey fans existed until his 45th birthday show at the Manchester Evening News Arena in 2004.

Morrissey has been back several times since, playing everywhere from the tiny Opera

House and Lowry, to two Christmas shows in 2006 at Manchester Central (the G-Mex to you and me). The two spring Apollo shows in 2009 to mark his 50th birthday were supremely special and celebratory. Could this Saturday hit the same heights?

Saturday 28 July 2012
Manchester Arena, England

And so the tenth and last Morrissey gig of this journey for me. Inverness, Dunoon, York, Bradford, Douglas, San Antonio, Austin, Dallas, Rome and Manchester. While the Texan dates involved travelling 4,000 miles, today I'm doing less than 40.

Kristeen Young has already upped the excitement on her Facebook page: she writes "Tonight it's Heeeeere, MANCHESTER ENGLAND Saturday July 28 (Manchester Arena) Can just feel how people are about to explode. I would even call it volcanic." I know how she feels. My head is gonna combust at the thrill I'm feeling. Morrissey live in Manchester. The last time I attended a Moz gig of this huge size and significance was that doomed Liverpool Echo arena show in 2009. A Saturday, a loyal northern crowd, people flying in from everywhere. I hope that's where the comparisons with Liverpool end.

I get the X2 bus into Liverpool to meet Matt. We are due on a lunchtime train for the 40 min hop to Manchester. I'm buzzing as I enter the Crown, the pub next to the Lime Street train station. But Matt doesn't share my enthusiasm: "In some ways I'm not as excited as I would be if we were off to see him in Aberdeen or somewhere like Grimsby." I see where he is coming from: "I know what you mean. After all the fab journeys we've had to see Morrissey, this is the shortest. And Manchester is unlikely to hold as many surprises as Dunoon or Dallas. But still Matt, Morrissey tonight in Manchester..."

Those super sleuths Latta and McCully get on our train at St Helens and the banter begins. We hop off at Manchester Piccadilly and the four of us check-in at the Macdonald Hotel. This hotel is huge, it's four star. Latta has sniffed out a bargain. It is fitting that we've saved the very best hotel for the tenth and last gig. Not that Matt is in any way impressed. He'd rather a £20 Days Inn-style motel miles from anywhere.

We join Latta and McCully in their room which overlooks the city. In keeping with it being July in northern England, it's raining. As Morrissey sings on the room's Bose sound system, Latta pulls out a bottle of Lanson champagne: "Let's raise a glass to Moz, cheers everybody."

I leave them early to go to the Manchester Arena to pick up the tickets for the show and see who is in the early afternoon queue. It's a who's-who of Morrissey apostles. The Kelly brothers from Dublin are here, Margaret Gonzalez is here; every imaginable accent can be heard outside the entrance to the venue.

Like all Morrissey gigs, there is a tension in the air. I still to this day cannot fathom this feeling. It's a familiar apprehension which isn't just felt by me. Kirstyn Smith, 26, from Edinburgh is scurrying around; there seems to be some issues over the queue list. Who is on it, who isn't on it. Kirstyn: "It's not a Moz gig unless I'm stressed out."

Peter Melis, from Belgium, is a veteran of 73 Morrissey concerts. Today he has good reason to feel nervousness. The fan had an horrendous experience outside Morrissey's concert at Brixton Academy last August. The concert (that I'd decided not to go to) was played against a backdrop of major civil unrest on the streets. As Peter tried to hail a cab after the show he was knocked to the ground by looters and suffered a broken right leg. He was to spend three nights in hospital and was unable to attend Morrissey's show the following evening. Consigned to a hospital ward, he turned to partner Katia and, with a hint of hope, said: "I suppose this means I won't be able to go to the Palladium gig tomorrow". Katia responded: "Forget the Palladium gig."

Today, despite his Brixton nightmare of one year ago, Peter is back in Britain for more Morrissey. He says: "Every gig is so different. I love his music and I love the contact Morrissey has with his fans. He's not an artist like anyone else. He's like..." Peter pauses, then looks to the sky, before finishing his sentence: "Morrissey is just...WOW."

The 41-year-old's main worry is whether his leg will stand up to a crazy dash to the stage when the Arena doors open in three hours time: "I've heard it's a long distance to the stage and I don't know if my leg will be ok. But I will try." Peter's not had much luck travelling to Morrissey shows. A trip to Athens in 2002 was bad enough when the gig was cancelled. But it turned even worse when his wallet was stolen in an Athens restaurant.

"I was so pissed off after paying for my flights and hotels...then the concert was cancelled. Then I go and get my wallet stolen later that night. I went to the police and just said: 'Get me out of here and back to Belgium'."

Despite that travel trauma, Peter returned to Athens when Morrissey rearranged the cancelled shows. And during the gig Morrissey looked right at Peter during *I Like You* and shook his hand. It felt like Morrissey knew what had happened the first time Peter came to Athens. There have been some tremendous highs for this fan following Morrissey. In 2009, when he travelled to the Manchester Apollo show he met his now girlfriend Katia at Salford Lads Club. Not for the first time on this trip I find a couple united thanks to Moz the matchmaker.

A fortnight ago, Peter met Morrissey in Antwerp and gave him a rare T-Rex album. Peter told him about the Brixton broken leg. Moz said: "I know your face". The singer hadn't heard of the incident. Peter: "Morrissey seemed very concerned about what had happened to me at Brixton. But then said: 'But it was a great show!'"

As is the way for a standing gig, the queue list is doing the rounds outside the Arena. This is for the diehards to make sure they get their place on the front rail. It is entirely self-policed and is not something arranged by either the venue or Morrissey's team. Today, Curtis Butler got here at 4am to stake his claim as number one in the queue. He seems to be the unofficial keeper of the list. I first met the 19-year-old on a ferry headed to the Isle of Man almost exactly a year to the day. On that journey Debbie and Gemma referred to him as "our boy".

Curtis has been pretty busy since that show. He's attended 27 Morrissey gigs so far this year including Vegas and Hawaii. I say "so far" because Curtis plans to return to America later this year to attend more Morrissey gigs. In total he's spent £13,000 following the singer in the last year. "I'd like to do 150 Moz shows," he says ambitiously, "Then maybe I will start to wind it down a bit."

I ask Curtis how he affords it all: "I have a good job and I take a lot of unpaid leave." Me: "But why so many shows?" Curtis: "It's just what I like to do. I love to watch Morrissey and I feel like I'm missing out if I don't see him."

Someone who has been to even more Morrissey shows this year than Curtis is Margaret Gonzalez. Here again, another queue, another hard floor, waiting. She says: "I've watched Morrissey 30 times in the last year but every time I see him it's like the very first time." But why the need for so many gigs? Margaret: "I have a hard time expressing myself but when I listen to Morrissey's lyrics it's like there's someone else feels exactly the same way."

Gessica Finaurini has been to 45 Morrissey gigs in seven countries. Dressed in denim, the 37-year-old Italian sits on the floor keeping her place in line. She says: "I feel like I'm missing out if I don't see him. I missed The Smiths because I was too young so I'm making up for it by watching Morrissey as many times as I possibly can."

Annelie, 25, from Berlin is here too. I stood next to her in Rome. Annelie is a relative newcomer compared to other fans. Tonight will only be the sixth time she's seen Morrissey. She arrived at 9:30am and has 21st position in the queue. She only started listening to Morrissey three years ago. Her first ever Moz gig was last year at York Barbican. She says, with an air of regret: "I've no idea why I left it so long to see him."

There are excited faces everywhere, each giving their own personal take on what Morrissey means to them. American, Carol Edden, 56, from New Jersey: "Tonight is number 40. I just love him. The music has been my inspiration. And it's his fans too, I enjoy hanging out with the fans."

Mum-of-two Giorgia Franchini, 41, has seen Morrissey 30 times: "It's difficult to put into words but watching Morrissey becomes addictive. I'm completely starstruck when I see him."

Chelsey Eden, 26: "I will keep going to Morrissey gigs as long as he's still going." Fergus, 47 from Dublin, has been a fan since 1984: "Some things stay constant in life. Morrissey is one of them. Once the gig starts, the hairs on the back of your neck stand up. And you make a lot of friends through following Morrissey who you don't meet anywhere else, apart from Morrissey gigs."

Pedro Gaspar, 40, has flown in from Portugal with his flag which has a picture of Morrissey. He is stood with Roisin Henderson, 18, from Dunfermline who says: "My dad saw The Smiths." The two fans only met one hour earlier - both instantly realised each was a fan so they've come to the gig together.

I head away from the venue to Shambles Square; a courtyard of bars in the heart of the city. There's a few Morrissey fans about, sheltering from the rain. Dan's here with his mate, Nick, and Moz fan, Nigel, who they met at last summer's Hanley gig. Nigel clutches the cassette inlay sleeve of *Vauxhall And I*. It contains Morrissey's signature. I think wherever Nigel goes, Morrissey's autograph comes with him.

Latta, McCully and Crist have been sampling Manchester's pubs and ales most of the afternoon. I join them for a few more at Sinclair's Oyster Bar which at £1.17 a pint,, is without doubt the cheapest pub in Britain. As it gets towards 8pm I encourage them to drink-up and head into the venue. No chance, there's drinking still to be done. Matt: "He won't come on stage until 9:15pm at the earliest. Why walk over there now?" Me: "I dunno. It's our last gig and all that, so I just want to get in. I'll meet you near the back - I'll be stood near the mixing desk."

I leave, dodge the rain and get inside. There are some fabulous new Morrissey teeshirts for sale. One is a photo of Oscar Wilde with the question: "Who is Morrissey?" Another tee sees Morrissey's head superimposed onto the body of a Manchester United player from the 1960s. Skilfully controlling the ball with his right foot, Moz storms forward, a last minute substitute for George Best. The shirt bears the MUFC logo but underneath it says "Mozza United". It's a great shirt, but if I wore that at Anfield I'd be accused of treason.

The Arena feels like a modern, characterless football stadium. Three tiers of seats sweep high, the flat floor area is reserved for standing spectators. It's like a giant car park. I'm not one to routinely criticise big modern venues but there is just no comparison between this and the intimate concert halls we've visited over the last 14 months: Bradford St George's Hall, Douglas Villa Marina, Dallas McFarlin Auditorium, then Rome - a modern venue done tastefully.

But I do have great memories of this venue. As I walk down the steep steps to get to the floor I glance around and reminisce about the great nights I've had here over the last 15 years: Radiohead, David Gray, REM, Paul McCartney, The Pogues. I get down to the standing area. It looks very full until you get halfway back where the crowd thins out. I stand way back by the mixing desk, happy to watch from afar. I wonder if Peter's leg stood up to the rush to the front? I spot fellow Liverpudlian Matt Jacobson. He's on his own and says: "I left my mates in the pub." "Me too." We laugh and toast absent friends.

For me, tonight is just about enjoying the gig. I'm not desperate to be anywhere near the front. I don't have to be within hand-shaking distance of Morrissey. I just want a good singalong and a dance. It's nice to be in position waiting for the concert to start as opposed to being in a pub outside.

The intro videos play. Suddenly a panic. I turn to Matt Jacobson: "Hang on a minute - intro videos? - New York Dolls? - What time is it? Morrissey will be due on stage in five minutes. But it's only 8:20pm." I pull mobile out of pocket fast and frantically text the lads: "Put your pints down, Moz is on in five minutes."

I seriously can't understand them wanting to lounge in a pub on a night like tonight. Ok, the ales might be triple the cost inside the Arena, but at least I know I won't miss any of the action. And here I don't even have to move to get served. Arena staff walk round with huge backpacks full of ale. Lagers are dispensed as we watch the last intro video.

The atmosphere builds during the last intro song: *Imperfect List*. It's 8:25pm, I can't believe Morrissey is coming on so early. And then 20,000 cheers as the Prodigal Son enters and stands in front of his people.

First song: *You Have Killed Me*. Second: *Everyday Is Like Sunday*. Third: *You're The One For*

Me Fatty. Fantastic hits delivered with passion; Manchester, have a bit of this. The reaction from a legion of followers is electric. I sing along to every single word as if these songs are the last I'll ever sing.

I can barely make out Morrissey, he is that far away. There's no big TV screen to help either. In fact, the presentation is distinctly dumbed down compared to the last time he played here. No Vegas-style neon with Morrissey's name in lights. Just Moz, the band and their music. All I have is the sound. And it's perfect.

I see a fan clamber on stage for a hug - it's Curtis Butler. A lovely, touching moment as he recreates Gemma's stage embrace with Morrissey in Douglas. Then, as has been customary during each gig, Moz hands the microphone to a fan. Amazingly, out of any of the 20,000 people he could have chosen, it's Peter Melis with the world in his hands. And the fan seizes his moment: "It was nice to meet you in Antwerp. Always you will be welcome in Belgium. I hope you enjoyed that rare T-Rex album I gave you?"

A gracious bow and nod from Morrissey. I hope this wonderful moment between fan and singer banishes Peter's Brixton nightmare forever. *I Know It's Over* has half the crowd in tears; *Please Please Please Let Me Get What I Want* has all the crowd in tears. *Still Ill*, the finale.

Once he has gone, the sweat drenched disciples re-emerge from the front. Everyone seems taken by a remarkable night. Latta and McCully show up. Latta is not taken by the remarkable night: "Average, Dickie. He was average."

Me: "Where's Matt?"

Latta: "He's in the pub."

Me: "What?"

Latta: "By the time we made it over here Morrissey had already done five songs. We queued for 15 minutes trying to get down to the floor, then they ran out of wristbands so Matt just told them to stick it."

We jump a cab to Rusholme's curry mile. Poppadoms and veggie kormas. Matt shows up and has a face like thunder: "I can't believe he came on stage so early. Saturday night, hometown show, and he comes on at 8:30pm. Not impressed."

Sunday 5 August 2012

I'm feeling the urge to book another trip. In October, Morrissey embarks on a 35-date American tour. Matt has forgotten all about his Manchester disappointment and is considering a return to Texas for Morrissey's Beaumont date in December.

I get a Twitter message from Jamie Skelton, the lad from Leeds who I met at the very beginning of this Moz odyssey: "@dickieFelton are you going to see Morrissey in New York this October? I could do with a travelling companion."

The problem is I only have five more annual leave days left so it's a question of meticulously planning where we go to maximise that time. If I went to the Big Apple I could squeeze in three Morrissey concerts. There are some mad places on the tour that look intriguing, Flint, Michigan followed by Chicago the next evening would be an adventure aboard the beloved Amtrak.

The theme of the last 15 months of Morrissey shows has been one of living life to the max and being with the people you love. And so we just booked it. Seven nights in Cala D'or, Palma. Just me, Jen and Frankie. Apartment with terrace, pool, play area and nearby beach. Ice creams, sandcastles and not a single Morrissey concert in sight.

The End

Manchester...

Interlude 9

Usually the honour is reserved for the glorious dead. In the UK several airports are named after the great and the gone: John Lennon (Liverpool), George Best (Belfast). There's even one named after a mythical heroic outlaw: Robin Hood (Doncaster),

In the US, almost every airport has a celebrity or luminary attached to it. The trend stretches far and wide, from John F Kennedy in the east (New York) to John Wayne in the west (Orange County). Europe too: Austria has Wolfgang Amadeus. In Italy there's Leonardo da Vinci and Marco Polo.

Airports named after cultural icons? Worthy or worthless? Is it just a flight of fancy to suggest Manchester International Airport be named after one of the city's most famous sons or daughters? Joy Division's Ian Curtis or Suffragette Emeline Pankhurst would be contenders.

But what about someone born on May 22 1959? Someone very much in the here and now. A Stretford boy who became one of the most influential artists of all time. "Manchester Morrissey International Airport". Gosh, it has a lovely ring to it.

...

Postscript

When I started this ten gig, 12,000 mile journey, I wanted to highlight the passion, colour and eccentricity of Morrissey's fan base. I needed to uncover their motivations for following a pop star such huge distances around the world. What I found was a group of people bound together not just by their love of a singer but by their love of life. Each fan making their own individual journey for their own reasons.

In Douglas, one fan was following Morrissey in memory of a fallen friend. In Inverness a hen party was marking the end of an era and the start of a new one. In Dunoon there were three generations of the same family sharing their passion together. In other places, fans were going to as many gigs as possible because they were making up for lost time. For some, seeing Moz was the fulfilment of a lifetime's dream.

I'm not sure I found eccentricity among Morrissey fans at all. On this journey I found his fans to be intelligent, witty, funny and passionate. If anything, it was the random people I met along the way who provided the surreal-ness: Kate Middleton-obsessed tourists on Inverness-bound trains, chavs from St Helens who stank of Old Spice, Dallas taxi drivers who thought they were Santa.

Over the 12,000 miles and ten concerts, I got the impression that Morrissey and his fan base were doing absolutely fine. It's just the rest of the world that's barking mad.

Dickie Felton, October 2012, Liverpool

Memories of Morrissey
Reflections at the end of the journey:

Matt Crist: "From Dunoon to Dallas, the Isle of Man to Manchester, not to mention Italy, Poland and a few others along the way; the tour offered everything I could have expected of Morrissey on the road and more. I only have to think about the great shows in Krakow and Inverness or driving up to York with a throat infection with the prospect of no hotel and sleeping in a car for the night, to remind myself why we do it. As always with Morrissey, you are always left wanting that little bit more and who knows, if the credit card and the man himself can keep delivering, there will be a next time, somewhere."

Jamie Skelton: "I'd had a pretty tough 12 months before the 2011 Morrissey tour. I'd lost my dad. I had been very low, and when the tour was announced I just decided to go. I had a bit of money saved up and thought I'd follow Morrissey to try and take a break from everything. That summer I followed Morrissey all over: Perth, Inverness, Glastonbury, Hop Farm, Grimsby. It was an amazing journey in so many ways. I'd been devastated with losing my dad. But during that eight weeks with Morrissey, my life turned around for the better. It was like I was a much stronger person. I know it sounds like a cliche, but it's true; music really can save your life."

Carol Edden: "Not only did my suitcase get delayed when arriving in Manchester, it also got lost on the way home. At both Manchester and Philadelphia Airports I described my suitcase as being black and white zebra print with luggage tag that said 'Morrissey'. The customer service agent asked me: 'Your luggage tag that says 'Morrissey'? Is that someone you were travelling with?' I said 'If only' and then had to explain who Morrissey is. She then asked 'If I have to open the bag to identify it what would be on top?'. My reply: 'A red teeshirt with a picture of Morrissey on it'. The suitcase showed up two days later. Morrissey saved my life and now he has saved my bag."

Renata Spinola: "When the three concerts in Brazil was announced I felt so sad. It's funny how a huge fan could feel sad about news her hero was coming to her country after 12 years apart. I live in the northeast of Brazil and the nearest city he would perform is 842 miles far from here. I had to take a plane in order to see him but how could I do that if I was nine months pregnant? None of our flight companies would allow me to fly unless I had a medical prescription. My doctor said he would never give me a prescription for that. I followed every move of the tour in Brazil through the internet and my friend used to call me during the concerts and I could listen to several songs live. That was awesome and make me feel a little better. One week later my beautiful son Antonio was born and I'm already planning his first Morrissey tour. Maybe in 2013 or 2014 with the new record."

Rowena Kelly: "I stood right at the front of the Douglas gig. I was only a couple of metres away from Morrissey. He performed exquisitely, soulfully and very dramatically. Let's just say I found love, peace and harmony on my voyage to the Isle of Man. Happy memories for the rest of my life."

Annelie: "The Manchester concert was just the most perfect. I'd never heard Morrissey sing *Please Please Please Let Me Get What I Want* before. My friend compared me to the fountain at Piccadilly Gardens because I cried so much. It's just the most beautiful song. I can't believe I've actually heard it live and in Manchester. I can die happy now."

Chris Wilde: "I've just seen a lad of about 10-years-old wearing a Morrissey shirt from this tour. His friends were all in baseball caps and silly shorts. But he stood out a mile - the outsider. Stay like that, son. You'll be ridiculed and the world won't listen, but who needs the world when you've got Morrissey?"

Dickie Felton

Dickie Felton was born in Liverpool in 1973. His first Morrissey concert came aged 17 in 1991 at Aberdeen Capitol Theatre (three trains, eight hours, 740 mile round trip, we stayed at Auntie Yvonne's house in Bridge of Don).

This is Dickie's second book. His first, "The Day I Met Morrissey" was released in 2009. It was a Piccadilly Records Top Ten Book of The Year and Waterstones 'Most Recommended' tome. It is still buyable from: *www.dickiefelton.com*

Photo by Mark McNulty

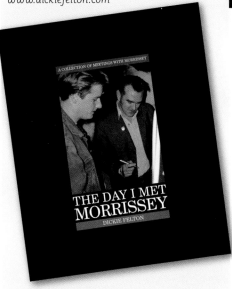

Acknowledgements

Thanks Morrissey and the band for ten amazing nights. Mum and Dad, Jen and Frankie for letting me go to so many shows.

Ta to Karen Miller, Clarkie, Kevin Rimmer, Marc Goodson, Mark McNulty, Sally Williams at BBC Inside Out and Merseyrail.

Special thanks to Matt Crist. We met outside Inverness Ironworks and ended up travelling together to Morrissey gigs from Dunoon to Dallas.

Robin Maryon designed this book and "The Day I Met Morrissey". He created the logo for Liverpool John Lennon Airport. It would be nice if Robin could design a new Moz-themed logo for Manchester International Airport some day.

For more banter:

Twitter: **@dickiefelton**
Web: **www.dickiefelton.com**

Justice for the 96. Don't buy the sun.